MW01273200

ONE NIGHT IN PARIS

City of Light Book 1

JULIETTE SOBANET

Saint Germain
press

ONE NIGHT IN PARIS
City of Light Book 1

Print edition published by Saint Germain Press 2020.

ISBN-13: 979-8630436009

Previously published by Amazon Publishing, StoryFront.

Juliette Sobanet's Free Starter Library

Sign up for Juliette's newsletter and receive three of her bestselling books for *free*. Details can be found on Juliette's website at *www.juliettesobanet.com*.

For Paris, my endless source of inspiration.

Chapter One

"*Y*ou're going to *Paris*?" Dave, my much older boyfriend, gapes at me as if I have two heads.

My tall heels click on the polished hardwood floors as I cross through the modern, museum-like living room of our New York City apartment, the stark white walls and constant chill in the air making me shudder. I pull my carry-on from the closet, doing my best to hide the trembling of my hands.

"My grandma is dying, Dave. She's the woman I was named after, and she wants to see me one more time before…" I swallow the knot in my throat and turn to him, searching for a hint of understanding in his cool hazel gaze.

Dave's heartstrings aren't so easily pulled, and as expected, my search for sympathy comes up empty.

He swirls the scotch around in his glass, then takes a long sip before leveling his deadpan gaze at me. "Ella, until tonight, I've barely ever heard you talk about this woman. And suddenly you have to drop everything to be at her bedside in Paris? It's only your second month at Campbell and Dunn—the firm *I* set you up with, in case you've forgotten—and you have a huge merger this week. I don't care who's dying, you're not leaving for Paris." He pauses as if he's waiting for an invisible jury to nod in approval.

"In case *you've* forgotten, you're not my boss anymore," I snap, thinking back to my very first meeting with Dave, when I was a summer associate at the corporate law firm where he had just made partner. Our booze-filled lunches turned into romantic weekend getaways…and as soon as I graduated and landed a position as a first year at his firm, Dave asked me to move in with him.

I was young, smitten, and naive when I said yes; I thought I understood what I was signing up for. More than the sweep-me-off-my-feet romance with an older, more experienced man, it was a lifestyle—a lifestyle I'd finally bought into after years of my parents, law school professors, and classmates all shoving it down my throat. Dave represented money, power, excitement, and a chance to join the ranks of a high-society partnership. My career at his firm set me on the path to making major deals that appeared in the *Wall Street Journal*, and my relationship with Dave meant that I was fully committed to the Manhattan work-till-you-drop-while-making-obscene-amounts-of-money lifestyle.

What I *didn't* understand when I jumped fully and squarely into the New York City rat race was that it's a recipe for emptiness, one that leaves me drained and utterly depleted at the end of each day. And seeing as how I don't have time to enjoy all of the money I'm making, let alone get a good night's rest, it's a race that has little to no payoff.

Ironically, my parents—*especially* my father—have never been more proud. And they *love* Dave.

But working for a man who holds a reputation as one of the most successful—and at times, one of the most vicious—attorneys in Manhattan, and then coming home to that same man night after night, has left me a little jaded, to say the least, which is why I recently decided to switch firms.

I thought the nausea I've been experiencing every morning before work and the chest pains that plague me every night when I return home would disappear as soon as I found a firm where I could forge my own identity, not one where I was constantly living in Dave's overbearing shadow.

I hoped the change would improve our relationship too—help him to see me as an equal, not as a younger, less experienced subordinate. I hoped we would remember why we first fell for each other and bring some pizazz back to this withering relationship.

But I was wrong. Nothing has changed, and in fact, I feel more suffocated, more exhausted, and more desperate than I've ever felt in my life.

The courage I need to leave has been building for months, but I still haven't built up quite enough strength to walk out the door for good.

The few times I've even hinted that a breakup could be in our future, my ultraconnected, all-powerful attorney boyfriend has made it ever so clear that if I walk out on him, I can say good-bye to my Manhattan law career too.

When a nurse called from Paris today, delivering the news that my beloved grandma Ella had taken a sudden turn for the worse in her battle against leukemia and isn't going to make it through the week, I suddenly couldn't have cared less about Dave's threats. I would've spent my entire life savings on a private jet if it would get me across the Atlantic quicker.

The predictably obstinate look plastered across Dave's face snaps me back to the present and reminds me of one more thing that is fueling my desire to escape: Dave *hates* losing.

"I may not be your boss," he quips, "but my best friend from law school is. You know he did us both a huge favor bringing you on. This isn't just about you, Ella. My reputation is at stake here too, just like it was back when we first started dating. With you switching firms, I thought those days were over. Apparently not."

At the mention of Dave's precious reputation, I feel a sudden and overwhelming urge to rip the ugly square vase off the equally dreadful square coffee table and hurl it at the wall.

Instead, I look him calmly in the eye. "It's a family emergency, and I'll be back in a few days. Life in Manhattan will continue to go on." I shrug off the nagging voice in the back of my head telling me that leaving Paris after only a few days may be just as difficult as saying good-bye to my grandmother.

He downs the rest of the scotch in one gulp as I roll my black suitcase right past him and into our bedroom.

Dave follows me to my overflowing closet, grilling me all the while; the stench of alcohol on his breath makes my stomach curl. "Jetting off to Paris during one of the biggest weeks of your career isn't going to impress anyone. Have you thought any of this through, Ella?"

The only things I'm thinking about at the moment are my beautiful grandmother, how many sundresses I'll need to pack for the humid summer air in her Left Bank apartment, and how quickly I can stuff them into this suitcase, catch a cab to the airport, and get the hell out of this smothering city to be by her side.

As Dave hovers over me, ready to fire more questions, I place a hand on his shoulder. "Of course I've thought this through, and I know it won't look good," I admit. "But this is really important to me. My grandma Ella is the only person in my family I've ever had a true connection with."

"Wait, isn't this the woman who's technically your *great-grandmother*?"

"Technically, yes," I say, annoyed that he feels the need to point out such an inconsequential detail upon hearing the news that someone dear to me is dying. "Her daughter—my *actual* grandmother—died when I was only five years old. Ever since then, Great-Grandma Ella became Grandma Ella… and honestly, she was more of a mother to me than my own mom."

I turn my back to Dave, not wanting to show him the tears that are gathering in the corners of my eyes. Tossing a pair of sandals into my suitcase, I harness my emotions and continue on. "In the summers between boarding school, my parents sent me to Paris every year to learn French with her. But it was more than a three-month French lesson…Those were some of the happiest times in my life."

A vivid memory of the two of us riding matching *bicyclettes* through the winding cobblestone streets of Montmartre flitters through my mind, making my heart ache. I still remember how vibrant Grandma Ella always looked with her elegant Parisian scarves blowing in the breeze as we'd stroll down the Seine, then meander through the Latin Quarter to pick up baguettes, *fromage,* and fresh flowers on our way home. Of course we almost never made it out of the apartment without a stop at Shakespeare and Company, the famous English bookstore situated perfectly on the Left Bank —an absolute treasure trove of history and charm, much like my grandma Ella herself.

How have I stayed away from her *and* from Paris for ten whole years?

"That's all fine and good," Dave snaps, "but this is real life, Ella. You can't just pick up and leave the country a month after scoring a position at one of the top firms in Manhattan. Not if you expect that position to be waiting for you when you return."

I know he's right, and I also know he intends that as a threat, but I ignore him all the same, throwing a stack of underwear into my suitcase.

Suddenly he wraps his fingers around my wrist, squeezing it so hard I can't help but let out a yelp.

"I won't let you do this, Ella," he growls.

I yank my arm from his grasp, and as I gaze into those hardened eyes of his—the eyes that only see value in status, money, work, and material possessions—I realize that if I don't want to look like him in fifteen years, it's time to go.

Chapter Two

*P*aris in the summertime is exactly how I remember it. Hot, beautiful, charming, and delicious.

I roll down the window in the back of the taxicab, enamored with the beauty of this city that I have somehow managed to ignore for ten long years.

Couples stroll hand in hand along the Seine while tourists snap photos in every direction. Kiosks speckled with vintage books and magazines line the *quai* while an artist sits leisurely on his stool, painting a stunning view of the river, its romantic bridges, and la Tour Eiffel off in the distance.

My exhausting eighty-hour workweeks, our fancy white-with-a-splash-of-gray apartment, and my epic fight with Dave all feel light-years away, as a whiff of buttery croissants and strong French coffee floats into the cab and puts a smile on my face.

As I spot the *boulangerie* my grandma used to take me to every morning during our lazy Paris summers together, I know we are close. I want to savor these last few moments before I see her, knowing that what is about to come is going to be difficult—perhaps the most difficult thing I've ever faced.

And that for a while, her passing may wipe out the beauty of this magical city.

I wouldn't have it any other way though; Grandma Ella truly was like a mother to me, walking me through the summers of my youth with a warmth that my own mother never possessed. During my teenage years, instead of my mom's harsh "Boys only want one thing" speech or the "If you get pregnant, I'll kill you" talk, Grandma Ella taught me the importance of valuing female friendships over boys... though she *may* have given me a lesson or two on the art of flirtation.

Grandma Ella *wanted* to spend time with me; she couldn't wait for me to arrive every June, and she dreaded my departure each fall. On the flip side, by the way my wealthy parents carelessly shipped me off to boarding school each year, as if I were nothing more than a package to be moved from place to place, it was clear that *they* didn't have any desire to pass their busy days with the likes of me.

So it is only right that I make this trip to be with this woman, who loved me so dearly, in her final moments. Especially after I've neglected to come visit her for so long.

I swallow my guilt as the cab pulls up to her elegant apartment building situated on the picturesque boulevard Saint-Germain, only a quick walk away from the Seine, Notre Dame Cathedral, and le Jardin du Luxembourg—just a sampling of the enchanting places she used to take me during my yearly three-month stays in the City of Light.

The minute I plant my feet on the sidewalk, breathe in that warm summer air, and take in the life buzzing all around me in this magnificent city, I feel an immediate sense of coming home.

The skinny cabdriver lifts my suitcase out of the trunk, and I hand him a nice wad of euros for his help.

"*Merci*, monsieur," I say, noticing how good it feels to

speak French again, to hear the language twirling through the streets, dancing to its own rhythm.

How long has it been since I've spoken French? I wonder as I roll my bag up to the tall red door, then punch in the building code out of muscle memory.

Thanks to my grandma's refusal to speak English with me when I visited, I was fluent by my third summer in France. I took advanced French courses all through college to keep it up, but then came the demands of law school, followed by Dave—who simply has no interest in traveling to France and would rather spend what little vacation he takes lounging on a beach somewhere, Blackberry in one hand, glass of tequila in the other. And finally came my life as an overworked associate at a top Manhattan law firm, where doing anything just for the fun of doing it is strictly prohibited.

The door clicks, and I hoist it open, remembering how heavy it used to feel to me as a little girl. I roll my suitcase down the dark hallway and climb into the minuscule elevator, a reminiscent giggle escaping my lips as I recall how hard I used to laugh every time we'd squeeze into this thing as it shook all the way to the top.

Forget speaking French. When was the last time I *giggled* over anything?

The elevator opens up to the sixth floor before I'm ready. I pause, trying to brace myself for the sight of my dear grand-mother. For the sight of the bruises that will be covering her arms—the bruises which, as the nurse explained, went unchecked for too long, blaring symptoms of the leukemia that is now stealing her life.

I force myself to power ahead. After all, she's waiting for me. She didn't ask to see my parents. She didn't ask to see my aunts or uncles.

She asked to see me.

I pull out the massive medieval-looking key that Grandma Ella had made for me and let myself into her apartment, trying to harness the sadness that is spilling over inside of me.

Inside the dimly lit foyer, I spot a gray-haired nurse rushing down the hallway toward me, a panicked look streaking across her face.

I drop my suitcase, praying that I'm not too late.

"Mademoiselle Ella?" she says, reaching for my hand.

I nod, unable to speak as she hurries me down the hallway toward my grandmother's bedroom.

A second nurse greets us at the door, and before allowing me in, she places her hands on my shoulders. "She's been asking for you all day," she says in French. "She's ready to pass, but she won't let go until she sees you. Please, mademoiselle, tell her she can go peacefully. She is ninety-nine years old. She's struggling, and it's time for her to rest." The nurse's eyes are red-rimmed and watery as she pleads with me.

"I'll tell her," I say quietly. "I promise."

The nurses give each other a silent, knowing nod before ushering me through the door.

Breezy white curtains frame tall, open windows that showcase the most breathtaking view of the rooftops of Paris. A warm breeze floats into the room and gently rustles the petals of the fresh flowers sitting on the tables on both sides of my grandmother's four-poster bed. She lies in the center, her eyes drawn shut, her breathing labored, her weathered, bruised hands trembling as they lie on the covers.

I rush to her side, sliding my hand over hers and kissing her gently on the forehead. "It's me…little Ella," I whisper in her ear as I blink away my tears. "I'm here now."

The rouge on her cheeks only slightly covers up the pale shade of gray that has taken over her skin.

I brush my fingers over the thin, wispy strands of silver hair that line her face and realize that ever since I've known her, she's had this same color hair.

But her forehead is clammy, and her hands are trembling even more fiercely now.

Why didn't I come sooner? The life I've built back home feels so empty now.

Before I can wallow in my guilt for another second, my grandmother's hand squeezes mine and her eyes flutter open.

"Ella," she whispers. "My little Ella." The rest of her body may be withering away with age, with illness, but the sparkle I remember in those pretty blue eyes of hers hasn't gone anywhere.

"I'm here now," I say.

"Ella, I need you…to…" She pauses, sucking in an arduous breath.

"Take your time," I tell her. "Whatever you need me to do, I'll do it."

She nods her head slightly to the left. "The chest, in the closet," she whispers in English, her voice so scratchy it's barely recognizable. "Get it out."

"The chest? The one you would never let me look inside when I was little?" I say, trying to smile.

She nods, squeezing my hand once more. "Hurry."

The nurses look on, confused, as I run to the closet and rummage through my grandmother's collection of dazzling high heels and chic French scarves, searching for the old wooden chest I remember so well.

Finally, I find the chest hidden underneath a lush violet quilt toward the back of the closet. It's not as big as I remember, and when I lean forward to test its weight, I discover it's not as heavy as it looks either.

Just as I am placing the chest on the creaky hardwood floor next to my grandma's bed, she points a shaky finger toward the nightstand.

"*La clé,*" she says, switching into French.

"The key?" I ask. "Here, in this drawer?"

Despite my grandmother's weakened state, I have never seen her eyes look so full of urgency.

Pulling the drawer open, I remove a tarnished gold key that glints in the sunlight as I hold it up for her to see.

"Open it," she instructs.

As I turn the key in the rusty lock, I have to jiggle it a few times before it clicks. Lifting the lid, I peer inside to find an old, tattered photo album and a red satin bag. I remove both items from the musty chest and present them to my grandmother.

"The album," she says, struggling even more now with each breath.

I sit next to her and peel the worn cover open. The first faded black-and-white photograph I set my eyes upon makes me gasp. I already knew I hold an uncanny resemblance to my grandmother when she was young, but the twenty something woman gazing back at me in this picture looks *exactly* like me. With her short blonde bob, her cheeky grin, and her almond-shaped blue eyes, she could pass for my twin. The flapper dress that hangs loosely from her slim figure and the feathers sprouting from her wavy hair date this photo to the 1920s, but otherwise, she could be me—today.

When I hold the album up for my grandmother to see, she points at the photo beneath the one I am gawking at. There is my grandma Ella again, looking as dazzling as ever in her headdress, beads, and feathers. She is surrounded by a group of friends—another young flapper to her left looking as glamorous as a movie star, with her long cigarette holder and flirtatious grin, and a couple of handsome men dressed in suits, holding drinks and cigars. This picture is only a snapshot of what life must've been like for my young grandmother in the Roaring Twenties—sexy, fun, and carefree.

But when I look over at the ninety-nine-year-old version of the happy woman in the photographs, she is blinking back tears. "Lucie," she whispers. "My best friend Lucie. It's my one regret. I can't rest until you go back for her."

Then she taps the page, so I turn it, and several yellowed newspaper clippings fall out, all with beautiful photographs of the woman who was standing next to my grandma in the photo and holding her long cigarette.

In a whisper, I begin reading one of the articles to my grandma. "Lucie Jones, beloved daughter, sister, and friend, found dead in her Manhattan apartment at the young age of twenty-three…" I trail off, chills slithering up my arms as I skim the rest of the obituary in silence, then tuck the articles back into the album.

Suddenly Grandma Ella grips my arm, and I am startled by the strength still left in those brittle hands of hers. "It was Max," she says. "He took her to New York. I tried to stop her, but I didn't try hard enough; I didn't understand how serious it was. Please go back for her, Ella. Don't let her go. You'll know the signs."

I pat her softly on the hand and force a shaky smile. "I'm so sorry about what happened to your friend Lucie," I say. "I won't let anything happen to her, I promise you. Now relax. You need to rest."

She shakes her head in protest, then points to the red satin bag. "The dress," she says. "You must put it on."

Inside the sack, I find a feathery black-and-silver headpiece, a pair of vintage black earrings, a string of black beads, and a flashy red flapper dress. Holding up the dress, I stare back at the photos of my grandmother that could be mistaken for me and realize that *this* is the same dress.

"Put it on, dear," she orders. "I can't rest until you put on the dress for me."

A quick glance around the room reveals that the nurses have slipped out to give us our privacy. Leaning forward, I kiss my grandma on the forehead and smile at her, willing my lips not to quiver. "Of course I'll put the dress on," I tell her.

I strip down to my underwear and slide the boxy dress over my head. Stealing a quick glance at the full-length mirror next to her bed, I find that it fits me like a glove. Not only do I look like my grandmother did, I am the same size as she was. When I hear a wheeze pass through her lips though, I hurry to put on the headpiece, earrings, and beads.

When the flapper-girl ensemble is complete, I turn to her, throwing my arms over my head to give a little "ta-da" in the hope of making her smile.

But she doesn't. Instead, she points at the closet. "Heels. You need my heels."

Scurrying over to her extensive high-heel collection, I pluck up a pair of glittery black heels that would go perfectly with this outfit. I slip them onto my feet and return to her bedside.

There are tears in her eyes this time, and a smile spreads across her wrinkled face. "Stunning," she says. "Ella, you'll knock 'em dead." Then she reaches for me, and I take her in my arms and hold her while tears stream down my cheeks.

I can't hold it in any longer.

I don't want to let her go.

"Grandma Ella, I'm so sorry I haven't been back to visit you these past ten years. My life in New York has been so crazy, but I want you to know that you have always been in my heart. Our summers together were the happiest times in my life."

She reaches up to brush away my tears, then cups my face in her hands. "Listen to me, Ella," she says, and I can see that she is calling up all of her strength to say whatever it is she is about to say. "You need to *live*. Truly live. That's my parting gift to you. You'll have one night. One night only, so don't waste it."

"Okay, Grandma," I say, saddened that the combination of leukemia and old age has taken away her clarity of mind.

Her eyes search the flapper dress I'm wearing before she

shoots a frantic look back up to my face. "The brooch," she orders in between labored breaths. "Put it on as soon as you find it, and promise me you'll save Lucie. I won't rest until I know you've saved her."

"I promise, Grandma Ella. I promise I'll save Lucie."

Her hands fall from my face, and her head plummets back onto the pillow as she smiles at me. "I'll be waiting," she whispers softly.

And then she closes her eyes.

My heart tears inside my chest as I take her hands in mine, thinking that this is it.

But when I lean closer, I am infinitely relieved to hear the breath still passing through her lips. Checking her wrist, I find that she still has a pulse, weak as it is.

I tuck a strand of her hair behind her ear, then stand from the bed to let her get some more rest. But just as I reach the full-length mirror, I notice that a piece of the flapper costume has dropped to the floor.

It's an old-fashioned sparkly red brooch—the brooch she just instructed me to find. I'm confused about where to put it, but when I notice an open space on my headpiece between the feathers, I decide that is the perfect spot.

As soon as I fasten the glittery pin to my blonde hair, I feel a strange urge to twirl around in front of the mirror.

I brush off the ridiculous notion. I'm not a little girl anymore. My grandma is dying. What is there to be twirling around about?

But soon another gust of hot summer air blasts through the open window, brushing past my cheeks and fingertips, and before I know it, I am twirling.

Glimpses of red, black, and silver flash back at me in the mirror as I spin faster and faster, just like I used to do as a child, before life got so demanding, so complicated, so painful. The Paris air in my grandmother's apartment comforts me like a pillow, the scents of roses, red wine, and freshly baked bread floating around me until I can barely remember the exhausting life I've left behind.

My grandma's words ricochet through my head with each step I take in her tall black heels.

"You need to live. Truly live."

I *want* to live. I don't want to walk around half-dead the way I have been these past ten years, going from my home cube to my work cube, charging an obscene amount of billable hours, as if someday my massive paychecks will buy me a better life. Letting my career control every minute of my day, to the point where I don't even have time to enjoy my life.

That isn't living.

My head is swirling now, and I can't see which way is up or down. I try to stop spinning, but my feet keep moving, my heels pounding into the hardwood floor. I twirl faster and faster until the flowers, the curtains, the paintings in my grandmother's beautiful bedroom blur around me like a streak of watercolors. My breath is quickening, my heart racing, and all of a sudden I hear her urgent voice once more.

"Promise me you'll save Lucie. I won't rest until I know you've saved her."

With that name swirling through my mind—*Lucie, Lucie, Lucie*—another blast of humid wind knocks into me, and in a flash, I am enveloped in darkness.

Chapter Three

A jazzy piano tune rings in my ears as my feet shuffle around in circles. My hands clasp something warm. It isn't the music or the spinning or the feeling of someone's hands wrapped around mine that wakes me with a start—it is the sound of my own uncensored laughter.

My eyes pop open, and I am shocked to find a man I've never seen before holding my hands and twirling me in circles as he laughs even harder than me.

"Ella, you're a fiery one!" he says before breaking into a wiry little dance where he swings his legs out to the sides while bouncing around and grinning at me like a drunken loon.

What in the—?

"Come on, Ella, don't stop!" he urges. But my feet stop moving, and I let go of his hands as pure bewilderment takes over.

How does this man know my name? And where the hell am I?

Turning around, I discover that we are in the center of a dance floor and couples are dancing wildly all around us—doing the same spastic old-fashioned dance. As I size up the vintage attire everyone is wearing, I wonder if I've crashed a 1920s-themed costume party where everyone just happens to know the Charleston. The women are wearing showy little flapper dresses, feathery headpieces, and beads, while the men sport wide-legged pants, gangster hats, vests, and ties.

The stench of booze and cologne mingles with the cigarette smoke swirling through the stuffy nightclub air, and even though the crowds bopping around on the dance floor look like the happiest group of people I've ever seen, I suddenly feel nauseous.

"Sorry, I'm not feeling well," I say to my mysterious dance partner before taking off through the masses.

"Ella! Baby, come back!" he shouts over the music, but the thrumming in my ears quickly drowns out the sound of his voice.

How did I get here? And who are all of these jubilant, liquored-up people?

Pushing to the edge of the room, I spot a door with a WC sign on the front. I rush past a crowd of giggling twenty something women with long cigarette holders dangling from their fingers. Vaguely, I notice that they are gabbing away in French as I blast through the bathroom door, slamming it closed behind me.

I rush to the tiny sink and begin splashing cold water on my face.

This has to be a dream. But I realize with a jolt that nothing in my life has ever felt so real, so raw, so alive.

On the other side of the bathroom door, the saucy piano music grows even louder, and horns chime in for effect, playing an old tune that I recognize from the summers I spent at my grandmother's apartment. It's a song she used to play on her ancient record player.

Grandma Ella.

As I continue drenching my face with water, my last moments with her come rushing back to me.

The chest, the old photos, her friend Lucie's obituary…
and *the dress*.

As I jerk my head up to look in the mirror, I find that my
short blonde hair is partially covered by the black and silver
feathers spouting from my grandmother's headpiece. The
ruby-colored brooch pinned in the center shimmers in the
dim bathroom light. Strings of long black beads hang from
my neck. I look down at the glitzy red flapper dress and black
heels I put on back in my grandma's apartment.

Her words to me before I landed *here* force themselves into
my befuddled mind.

"You'll have one night. One night only, so don't waste it."

I think of the man on the dance floor who just called me
Ella. And I remember how the photos of Grandma Ella in her
youth are a spitting image of *me.* He easily could've mistaken
me for her—that is, *if* I am actually in the 1920s…

And in the second photo I saw—the one where my young
grandma was surrounded by her friends—*this* is the same
dress she was wearing.

Panic overtakes me as I grip the side of the sink. This isn't
possible.

It simply *is not* possible.

Have I traveled back to the 1920s to be her for a night?

No. This is ludicrous. I splash more water on my face,
hoping it will wake me up from this dream, or whatever the
hell this is.

But no matter how many handfuls of water I splash over
my burning cheeks, I can't find any other logical explanation
as to how I went from twirling around in front of my grandmother's full-length mirror to dancing with a stranger in the
middle of this booming jazz club—in what appears to be Jazz-
Age Paris.

A loud pounding on the door startles me so much I
almost slip on the water I've splashed all over the bathroom
floor.

"Ella! Are you in there?" a female voice shouts before the door bursts open.

The young woman gaping at me in the doorway has wavy jet-black hair bobbed to her chin, pale skin, and cherry-red lips. Her black dress hugs her petite frame, not leaving much to the imagination.

"What have you done to your face? And your hair?" she shrieks. "You're soaking wet!" She scurries inside, letting the door slam behind her as she rushes over to me.

"I…I…" I begin, but nothing more will come out. This glamorous twenties girl—*she* is the one from my grandmother's photos. And from the faded newspaper articles describing her gruesome death.

"Lucie?" I say. "Is your name Lucie Jones?"

"For crying out loud, Ella, how much rum did you drink?" She shakes her head at me, her pretty porcelain features scowling in disapproval.

"Too much, apparently," I mumble under my breath, wishing it were only that simple.

"Here, hold my ciggy." Lucie hands me her cigarette holder before she goes to work on my hair. "You can't expect to meet a man if you go out there looking like a ragamuffin. We've only been in Paris for a month—do you really want all these cute expats and French boys to think you can't hold your liquor? Now hold still while I fix you up right."

She swirls around me, repositioning my headpiece and combing her fingers through my short blonde waves. Then she grabs a cloth from the sink and dabs at my eyes before gazing perplexedly at my feet. "When did you get so tall? Did you switch heels before we left tonight?"

"I…um…yes?" I stammer.

She arches a brow at me as she tosses the towel back onto the sink and plucks her cigarette from my hands. "Your voice sounds different too. But I'm sure that's just the alcohol talking." She giggles, then continues gabbing. "Jean-Philippe looks *so* handsome tonight I could just die. I can hardly believe I met him only three weeks ago at this very jazz club! Don't you think he looks smashing?"

I barely hear her. My grandmother's words are flooding back to me, and although they didn't make any sense at the time, I can hardly ignore the bizarre, unbelievable reality staring me in the face.

I have to know for sure though.

Placing a clammy hand on Lucie's shoulder, I look her square in the eye. "Lucie, what's today's date?"

She breaks into another fit of giggles. "Ella, what on earth has gotten you so balled up?"

Balled up?

"Please, Lucie, I'm serious. Just tell me today's date."

"Why, it's June 12, 1927, and we're in Paris having the time of our lives. Has the alcohol really made you forget *everything*?"

As Lucie takes my hand and leads me out of the bathroom and back into the smoky jazz club, I want to tell her that no, I haven't forgotten everything—especially not my grandmother's final words to me.

"Promise me you'll save Lucie. I won't rest until I know you've saved her."

Chapter Four

*A*s I trail Lucie to the bar, I wonder how on earth I'm going to accomplish the monumental task of saving her life.

"Lucie!" I call over the music, but she isn't paying any attention as she hoists one hip onto the barstool. With a bat of her long eyelashes, she summons the bartender.

"What can I get for you, sweetheart?" he asks in French.

I grip her elbow, about to tell her that we don't need any more drinks and we really ought to leave—or more appropriately, I need to stop her from ever moving back to New York, then promptly find a way back to the twenty-first century—but a male voice cuts me off.

"Une bouteille de champagne pour les deux jolies filles."

Turning to see who has just ordered a bottle of champagne for us—*the two pretty girls*—I find a tall, dark, and *very* handsome Frenchman brushing past me to get to Lucie.

"There you are, doll," he says in a thick accent as he slides an arm around her waist. "I thought I'd lost you."

"Never, Jean-Philippe!" she says, flashing him a sexy grin.

Lucie wasn't lying earlier in the bathroom. With his spiffy

pin-striped suit, his shiny red tie, and that charming grin, Jean-Philippe is *quite* the looker.

"*Bon,*" he says, kissing her on the cheek. Then he turns to me. "Ella, I saw you leave the dance floor in quite a hurry earlier. *Ça va?*"

I want to tell this dashing Frenchman that everything *is not* okay.

But Jean-Philippe's question is so genuine, his eyes so sincere, that I am certain my truthful response will only make him think I'm a lunatic—and rightfully so.

So I nod and smile. "Oh yes, everything's just fine."

Three tall glasses of champagne appear on the bar, and Lucie and Jean-Philippe snap theirs up, waiting for me to do the same.

I eye the bubbly alcohol, realizing that I haven't had a taste of champagne in years—after all, champagne is reserved for celebrations, and there simply hasn't been time to celebrate anything in my nonstop life back home. Dave pretty much always has a glass of scotch in his hand, but that's just par for the course with his live-to-work-and-wash-away-your-troubles-with-alcohol lifestyle. He's not big on celebrating much of anything these days except a major case win or one of his outrageous bonuses. But in this moment, suddenly a long way from *that* life, I figure a sip of champagne won't hurt. If anything, it will sooth my frazzled nerves.

I pick up my glass and raise it to meet theirs.

"To a swell night in Paris," Lucie says as we all clink glasses.

"To a swell night," Jean-Philippe echoes in his endearing accent.

As the fizzy alcohol slides down my throat, I feel an ounce of comfort. But when Jean-Philippe sweeps Lucie off her stool and leads her onto the dance floor, I realize that a little bit of champagne is not going to solve my problems right now.

I've only just met Lucie, but I can already tell she is smitten with Jean-Philippe, and convincing her to leave this jazz club so I can have a proper talk with her is *not* going to be easy.

Even if I could sit her down to talk, what would I say?

"I come from the future. I'm not really the same Ella you think I am—I am her great-granddaughter—and the real Ella sent me here to save your life."

Yeah, that would go over real well.

With one hand on the bar, I close my eyes for a moment, trying to think this through.

"You look lost."

A deep male voice travels over the lively jazz music and snaps me out of my daze. A young man with dusty-blond hair and boyish blue eyes is leaning against the bar right next to me and shooting me a curious grin. The top button of his white collared shirt is open, and the gray vest he's wearing is a little snug around his chest.

He waits patiently for me to pull my eyes from his chest.

"Lost? You could say that," I respond, embarrassed, before taking a long sip of champagne.

When I resurface for air, his hand is outstretched.

"Let me help you find your way," he says. "I'm Leo Knight. American, a writer…well, aspiring writer. You?"

I slip my hand into his, noticing how warm it feels. How comfortable.

"Ella Carlyle, and I…I'm…" I pause, realizing I can't tell this guy who I *really* am. So instead, I tell him what I always wanted to be when I was growing up, what I trained to be *before* my lawyer parents told me they wouldn't support such an impractical career. "A ballet dancer," I finish. "And I'm American too."

I catch those inquisitive blue eyes of his running up and down my legs. "You've certainly got the gams for the ballet, if you don't mine me saying so, miss." He twirls his gray cap around on one finger, his warm grin revealing a dimple in his left cheek. "And the face for it too. Ballet dancers have the prettiest faces. But yours…well, I've never seen anything quite like it."

A flush that starts at my toes creeps all the way up to my cheeks, surely turning them the color of a strawberry in summer. I'm not usually this susceptible to pickup lines, but this guy is such a breath of fresh air compared to the hard-edged Manhattan types back home—he's got charm and charisma, and to be honest, I've never seen anything quite like him either.

How did the women of this era get anything done with all of these gorgeous men popping up around every corner?

Catching a glimpse of Lucie and Jean-Philippe bopping around on the dance floor like two lovesick teenagers, I remind myself that this isn't the time to get wrapped up in my own schoolgirl crush. I've got two important tasks to accomplish. And although I'm not 100 percent certain what *exactly* those tasks entail other than protecting Lucie and hoping that in doing so, I will find a way back to my grand-mother's bedside, I am certain that flirting with this hand-some stranger isn't going to get me closer to either.

Leo pushes off the bar, then fastens his cap atop his head. "Care to let me take you for a twirl out on that dance floor, Ella Carlyle?"

"No, really, I can't," I say, but Leo takes a step closer to me, the scent of his cologne and the proximity of his tall, firm body making me regret my answer.

"Oh, I see what's going on," he says with a sly grin.

He's so close now that his warm breath is tickling my lips. I should turn and walk away. I need to watch out for Lucie. But a tiny part of me—the part that has been yearning for something new, something different, something exciting to happen in my life—speaks up.

"What's that?" I ask, shooting him my own flirtatious smile.

"The ballerina doesn't think a writer from Saint Louis has any moves." He offers me his hand once more. "Let me prove you wrong, Mademoiselle Ella."

Peering over my shoulder at Lucie, who is now wrapped tightly in Jean-Philippe's arms, I figure just one dance won't hurt anything. It will buy me a few minutes to think, to figure out my next move.

"Deal," I say, giving Leo my hand.

Just before we reach the dance floor, I lean into Leo's ear and whisper. "I have a confession to make. I don't know how to do the Charleston."

"A ballet dancer who doesn't do the Charleston," he says, his eyes lighting up with the challenge. "Well, I never."

"I don't get out much," I admit. "Not to places like this, anyway." *If he only knew.*

"Well, Miss Ella Carlyle, tonight is your lucky night." Leo winks at me as he ushers me onto the dance floor.

With his hand around my waist and his body pressed closely to mine, I realize it's not likely I'll get much *thinking* done during this dance.

Chapter Five

"*L*et's start with the feet, and the arms will follow," Leo instructs over the flashy jazz tune. The pianist and horn players are belting it out in the corner of this club.

He takes my hands and swings his legs out to the sides, slowly at first, nodding me for me to do the same.

As I begin to pick up the moves, I lift my gaze to find Leo grinning back at me with the sweetest, most carefree smile on his face—a smile that momentarily makes me forget what I'm supposed to be doing with my feet.

Or what I am supposed to be doing *here*, in a jazz club in the 1920s.

For the briefest of seconds, I wonder what it would be like if I could take Leo back with me. A smile that nice—and that charming—would surely erase the gray clouds that have taken up permanent residence over my life in New York.

"A little faster now," Leo says, speeding up his pace as he moves my arms from side to side.

I lower my focus back to his feet, trying to mirror his steps instead of swooning over those big blue eyes of his.

"Attagirl!" he says. "Now turn."

Leo twirls me around, his hand tracing my waist as I spin. I barely recognize the feeling surging up through my chest, the feeling making me smile unabashedly at him despite the fact that we've only just met.

It's something resembling happiness—but I haven't felt anything like this in so long I'm hesitant to place a label on it.

Whatever it is, I like it.

For the second time tonight, I hear myself giggling, the laughter pouring from inside of me as if I haven't laughed in years. Leo laughs with me as he clasps both of my hands once more, our fingers intertwining while we hop around the dance floor together.

The excitement in this place—and in Leo's eyes—is contagious. I know I should be frightened over my mysterious voyage back in time and focused on making it back to present-day Paris, but with this vibrant American writer showing me how to do a dance I've never done before, I cannot ignore the exhilarating feeling coursing through me.

I feel *alive*.

A flash of me hustling through the concrete jungle of Manhattan invades my mind. I see myself answering e-mails on my Blackberry while I rush to the subway, guzzling Starbucks all day to make it through my insanely long work days, then pretending to fall asleep before Dave returns home at night so I don't have to deal with him rambling into the apartment drunk after late dinners with clients—clients who occasionally leave lipstick stains and traces of perfume on his dress shirts.

Leo spins me around once more, snapping me back to my present moment. I shake away the memories, pushing them far, far out of my mind.

If I only have one night here, as my grandmother said, I don't want to waste it thinking about my past—or my *future*, rather.

As the lively tune comes to a close, a woman steps up to

the microphone, then winks at the pianist. He tips his black hat at her, then traces his fingers over the keys, whipping up a slow, sultry tune.

The glamorous young singer joins in, her voice deeper and louder than I expected, and rich with pure, seductive emotion. Her busty chest and swaying hips catch the eye of every drooling, excited man lined up at the bar.

But there is one man whose attention is *not* glued to the sexy jazz singer belting out her love song—*Leo.*

His baby blues are fixed on me.

He moves in closer, one hand wrapping tightly around my waist as he whispers in my ear. "I'm assuming Ella the ballet dancer knows how to dance slow?"

His strong hands send butterflies dancing through my stomach.

I nod, letting him scoop me up into his arms. The alluring scent of his cologne mixes with those few sips of champagne I took, making me feel light-headed and tongue-tied all of a sudden.

Leo sweeps me around the dance floor, and for the next few minutes, I am totally lost in him. That nagging voice of reason in the back of my mind—the one that has been in charge for *way* too long now and, I'm only just realizing, sounds like a mixture of Dave and my father—tries its damnedest to snap me out of my haze and steal away this moment of happiness.

But another voice is stronger, more powerful than my own —my grandma Ella's.

"You need to live. Truly live. That's my parting gift to you."

I can almost hear her whispering those words in my ear as Leo spins me around and pulls me close. Even though she is so close to passing, my intuitive grandma must've known that this would be just the jolt I need to get my confidence back, to reclaim my *own* voice.

And so I allow myself to unravel, to be exposed, to be *alive* in Leo's arms.

"I'm awfully glad I met you tonight, Ella Carlyle," Leo says, his chest pressing into mine as we sway together to the music.

"I'm glad I met you too, Leo Knight," I say, marveling at how much younger I feel, and how much lighter too. As if I've dropped a weight the size of the Empire State Building— or more appropriately, the Eiffel Tower—from my shoulders.

Leo's fun-loving grin and that exciting spark in his eyes hold me captive as he speaks. I've never known that spark in Dave, or in any other man for that matter. "Ella, I hope you don't mind me being so bold, but after this night is over, I hope I get to see much more of you."

His forward words are the most romantic ones I've heard in a long time—maybe ever. But they are also an unwelcome reminder of my perplexing situation, of the fact that I don't know how I arrived or if I'll even be here when the sun comes up tomorrow. As I gaze up into that handsome face of his, realizing he would kiss me right now if I let him—and my God, I know that kiss would be smoldering—I know I simply can't go there.

"Leo, I'm sorry. There's something—"

But a commotion at our backs stops me midsentence.

Whipping around, I spot Lucie toward the back of the club, crying and yelling as she tries to pull a big, burly man off of Jean-Philippe.

"Lucie!" I call out, pushing past a group of bewildered flapper girls to reach her.

"Ella!" Leo shouts after me as he follows close behind.

The bartender is one step ahead of both of us. He lunges at the man punching Jean-Philippe and tries to separate the two men, but the beast delivering the beating is too strong for him. He knocks the bartender away in one swift blow and continues pounding poor Jean-Philippe.

"Leave him alone, Max! He didn't do anything!" Lucie shouts as tears stream down her cheeks. "Max, please stop!"

As my eyes zoom in on the dark-haired brute of a man whose fist is doing a number on Jean-Philippe's chiseled face, the name hurling from Lucie's lips rings a sudden bell.

Max.

How could I have forgotten? After I tucked Lucie's faded obituary back into the old photo album, my grandmother warned me about him.

She said not to let Lucie leave Paris with him—that I would know the signs.

Was *this* the man responsible for Lucie's death?

Judging by the way this lunatic refuses to stop his vicious assault on Jean-Philippe, the signs are pretty clear. Max is up to no good, and if he's that quick to harm someone Lucie cares about, it's likely he'll be just as quick to harm Lucie.

Just as I am about to pull Lucie away from the brawl, Leo jumps in and socks Max in the jaw, creating an uproar in the rowdy mob gathering around us. A mixture of French and English cries fly past my ears, but I barely hear them as Max's stony gaze fixes on Leo.

Leo doesn't back down. Instead, he strips off his vest, tosses it into the crowd, then clenches his fists and raises his chin at Max, a silent and bold invitation to come closer.

For a second, Max is torn between Jean-Philippe—still writhing beneath him, bleeding from the nose—and his new rival, the young writer from Saint Louis who is about two-thirds his physical size but clearly hasn't a cowardly bone in his body.

Lucie lunges forward, shocking us all as she wraps a tiny arm around Max's neck. "That's enough!" she shrieks. "It's over!"

Max snatches Lucie's arm from his neck, then stands, releasing Jean-Philippe.

I expect Lucie to fawn all over Jean-Philippe's mangled

face, but she doesn't. Instead, as a few young flapper girls rush to his side, Lucie turns and bolts toward the back of the club, tears streaming down her face.

"Lucie! Baby, come back." Max has already forgotten about Leo's punch and is hot on her heels, yelling for her over the crowd.

As the jazz music picks up right where it left off, adrenaline pours through me. I have to stop Lucie from going anywhere with this monster. I weave through the dance floor, which immediately fills again with couples who continue smoking, drinking, and dancing the night away.

Max's tall frame slips into the bathroom behind Lucie, and before I can reach them, he's already closed the door. I jiggle the handle, but it's locked.

Pressing my ear against the door, I try to block out the sounds of laughter, piano, and horns bouncing through the club and focus instead on Max's and Lucie's voices.

"Lucie, baby, I'm so sorry. Come here," Max says, his tone both desperate and powerful.

"What are you doing in Paris, Max?" she cries. "Why didn't you tell me you were coming?"

"Sweetheart, I wanted to surprise you. I wanted you to see how things have changed. I'm a different man now."

"Then why did you attack Jean-Philippe? He didn't do anything to you."

"I'm sorry, baby," Max says. "I don't know what came over me. I saw that man's hands on you, and I...I still love you. I can't stand seeing you with someone else. You don't really love that Frenchman, do you?"

"He treats me well. He makes me feel like a lady. He's silly, and we have fun together." Lucie pauses, then lowers her voice so that I can barely hear her next sentence. "And we don't fight the way you and I did."

"But would he travel all the way across an ocean just to tell you he loves you?"

When Lucie doesn't respond, Max keeps talking, trying to put on a sincere show, but I can smell his bullshit through the bathroom door.

"Give me a second chance, and I'll prove to you that I've changed," he pleads. "I even stopped drinking just for you, my sweetheart. Those times when I…when I hurt you…well, I've never forgiven myself. It will never happen again. I promise you that."

A memory of my last night with Dave in our New York apartment flashes through my mind. I can still feel his fingers wrapping around my wrist, smell the stench of alcohol on his breath. He didn't hit me *that* night, but once, in the heat of an argument only a few months ago, he'd shoved me against the wall.

Just like Max, Dave had apologized, promised it would never happen again.

I believed Dave at the time—or rather, I *wanted* to believe him. But the other night, when he grabbed me and forbade me to leave for Paris, I saw the same look in his eye that I noticed in Max's tonight.

I never would have believed it when I first laid eyes on Lucie in the bathroom earlier, the little spitfire that she was, but it seems we have more in common than I originally thought.

Lucie *wants* to believe Max. Otherwise, she wouldn't still be locked in the bathroom with him.

"Come back to New York with me," Max says. "I'll even buy you your own apartment in the city until you're ready to get married, have kids. I'll give you the life you've always dreamed of. The bad times are over, baby. I know you still love me. I can see it in your eyes. That Frenchman can't give you what I can. Come home with me."

I hear Lucie sniffling.

"Oh, baby, don't cry."

If Max calls her "baby" one more time, I swear I'll bust

through this door. Can't Lucie see that he's lying? That he's a selfish, abusive man who will make her miserable? A man who, if my grandmother is right, will *kill* her.

It seems so clear as the outsider looking in, but I cut Lucie some slack. I know what it's like to be in her shoes. And with the exception of my mysterious voyage back in time, I still *am* in her shoes—I haven't actually broken up with Dave, after all.

In fact, he thinks I'll be coming home to him in a few days…

"Oh, Max. I've missed you so much. I can't believe you came back for me." Lucie's soft, broken voice snaps me back to the present.

When I think back to the obituaries that my grandmother kept tucked in her picture album all these years, I know that when this happened the first time around, Max's pathetic attempt must've swayed Lucie enough to leave Paris and move back to New York with him. He must've bought her that apartment in Manhattan—the apartment in which he eventually took her life.

According to the faded clippings, Lucie was only twenty-three when she died. She couldn't be much younger than that tonight. Max didn't even give her the chance to get married, to have kids, as he just promised. Instead, he left her beaten and stabbed in her apartment, where she died alone. The articles mentioned that the killer was never identified, which means that Max walked away free and clear. The sick bastard.

As I remember my grandmother's urgent plea to save Lucie, I know I cannot allow this young, vulnerable woman to make the wrong choice. I must stop her from leaving with Max.

"Lucie!" I call as I pound on the door. "Lucie, it's Ella. Unlock the door."

"She's fine," Max responds, half growling.

"Why don't you let the lady answer for herself," Leo calls

out as he slides up beside me. His knuckles are red and swollen from the punch he threw Max, but he doesn't seem fazed in the slightest. In fact, by the fiery look in his eyes, I'm certain he would have no problem doing it again if need be.

"Is she okay?" Leo mouths to me.

"No," I say quietly, shaking my head.

"Lucie, I need to talk to you," I shout through the door. "It's important. Come out of the bathroom *now*." The force in my own voice surprises me, but I won't back down.

Finally the handle jiggles and the door swings open. There stands Lucie, her mascara smudged underneath her pretty eyes, her lips quivering as she tries to put on a smile. "Everything's fine," she says with a sniffle. "It was all a big misunderstanding, and Max has apologized to me, so there's nothing to be concerned about."

"That's my girl." Max slides a muscular arm around Lucie's waist and kisses her forcefully on the cheek. "Let's get out of here, sweetheart. I got us a nice hotel room on the Left Bank."

"Lucie isn't going anywhere with you," I tell him. I don't care that the barbarian standing in front of me bears a striking resemblance to the man waiting for me back in New York. A switch has gone off inside me, and I'm not afraid anymore.

Just as Max opens his mouth to fire his retort, I cut him off.

"I need to speak with Lucie. You are going to get the hell out of this club, out of this *city*, and leave Lucie alone," I order.

When Max's angry eyes flash at me, Leo steps forward. "Why don't we leave the ladies alone for a minute? You and I can take a little walk outside, get some air. What do you say?"

I shoot Leo a questioning glance. Does he really want to be alone with this man?

Leo's firm stance shows nothing but confidence as he stares the bully down, and to my surprise, Max concedes.

"Fine." Max turns to Lucie, planting a hard kiss on her lips.

Leo pulls me to the side, whispering in my ear. "Don't worry. I know how to handle him. Meet me out front in ten minutes, and bring Lucie, okay?"

"Are you sure?" I ask him.

Leo squeezes my shoulder as the corners of his lips curl up, revealing that sexy grin. "Trust me, Ella Carlyle. I've seen the likes of this fella before. It's under control."

Chapter Six

*A*s Max follows Leo out of the bathroom, I reach for the towel. It's my turn to clean Lucie up.

She's still sniffling as I wipe at the makeup smeared down her pale cheeks. "Lucie, that man is no good," I tell her.

"He promised me that he changed," she says, but I can hear the doubt lining her voice. "You know that's all I wanted for so long. What if he's telling the truth? What if things could be different with him now?"

"What about Jean-Philippe? He's clearly smitten with you, and you've been having so much fun with him. You can't just leave him behind for that savage. Especially after what happened tonight."

"Max just got a little jealous, that's all," Lucie says. "And he's offering me so much more now. An apartment in Manhattan, and someday marriage, and even children. What if this is my one chance to have all of that, to have a family, and I give it up?"

"Lucie, you're young, fun, and gorgeous. And you just moved to Paris, the most romantic city in the world. You couldn't possibly think that Max is your only shot at having a family one day. And besides, are you even ready for all of that? We're having so much fun in Paris, why would you want to leave all of this for someone who's hurt you so badly?"

"Max did hurt me…but he loves me," Lucie says. "And he wants another chance. Would it really be so bad to give it one more try? He said he's a changed man, that he's stopped drinking. If I turn him down, I'll always wonder if we could've had a happy life together."

I think back to Lucie's beautiful photograph at the top of her faded obituary, and to the vicious look on Max's face as he beat the hell out of Jean-Philippe only a few minutes ago.

Tossing the towel back onto the sink, I level a serious gaze at my grandmother's best friend, instantly recognizing the look in her eyes—not hope or true love, but fear. And even though I don't want to admit it, it's a look—or rather, a feeling—that I know all too well.

"Yes, it will be *that bad* if you give Max one more chance," I say sternly. "You need to trust me on this. Men like Max *do not* change. He will be the end of you. I mean it."

Lucie nods slowly, giving me the notion that deep down, she already knows that what I'm saying is true—she just isn't strong enough to admit it in the face of that overbearing man.

"But what will Max do if I break the news that I'm staying in Paris? He's come all this way just to see me, to ask me back. Even if he has changed, he clearly hasn't lost his temper. Poor Jean-Philippe learned the hard way."

"I promise you, Lucie, I will not let you out of my sight tonight," I say firmly. "You have nothing to worry about. And in fact, I think Leo is taking care of Max as we speak."

Lucie's face freezes in panic as she grips my arm. "I thought he was just taking Max outside to make amends. Was he taking him out there to fight?"

"No, I think Leo's just having a talk with him, trying to calm him down—" But Lucie doesn't let me finish. Instead, she pushes past me, the flaps of her slinky black dress disappearing in the waves of smoke still billowing through this Roaring Twenties joint.

"Lucie!" I call as I spot her jet-black bob bolting through the front door.

I dodge two young Frenchmen doing their best to woo a set of identical flapper twins with their most animated dance moves, and rush past them through the door.

Outside, the humid night air envelops me like a glove as I search the winding alley for Lucie. A dim lamppost at the corner of the street reveals her charging toward Leo and Jean-Philippe, who are pinning Max to the side of the building. From what it looks like, they're giving him quite the "talking to."

"You don't even love Lucie," Jean-Philippe says before any of them notice Lucie approaching. "If you loved her, you never would've laid a hand on her."

"Who said anything about love?" Max spits. "Lucie's my woman. She *belongs* to me, and I'll put my hands on her any way I please. I'll be damned if I let some dirty Frenchman do the same."

Lucie stops in her tracks, her hand shooting to her heart. I catch up to her, and instead of the tears I'm expecting to see in her eyes after Max's cruel remarks, a new fire blazes. She squares her shoulders, places her hands on her hips, and marches up to Max.

The second Max sees her, he shakes off the two men and reaches for Lucie.

"Baby," he starts, but Lucie cuts him off with a hard slap to his smug face.

Leo, Jean-Philippe, and I are too stunned to say a word.

Lucie pauses for a moment, her hands shaking at her sides, but she quickly regains composure and charges at Max.

"Who said anything about love?" she shouts. "If I'm not mistaken, *you* just did, in the bathroom, only five minutes ago! I've had just about enough of you. Right when things are

finally starting to look up for me, you race over to Paris and act like you're saving me from something. Well, I have news for you, Max. I don't need to be saved by you. I never did, and I certainly don't now."

Judging by the dumbfounded look in Max's eyes, he's never witnessed this kind of unwavering confidence from the sweet little Lucie he used to knock around for fun.

Lucie isn't fazed by his silence. Instead, she smacks his bruised cheek again.

"That's for hurting someone I care about. It's over between us, Max. I don't want your fancy Manhattan apartment. I don't want your engagement ring or your children." Her voice quiets down now, and from the soft lamplight outlining her profile, I can see that she is holding back tears. "I loved you once, but you ruined that. And you can't have it back. I'm happy here in Paris with Ella and Jean-Philippe. So please, just go."

Max shakes his head, rubbing his bruised jaw with his hand. "Fine. If you say the word, I'll leave you alone. Forever."

Lucie hesitates, her lips trembling as she catches my glance.

I nod at her, infusing as much confidence and strength as I can muster into my silent message. *Let him go, Lucie. He'll only hurt you.*

She nods back, and her mouth ceases its quivering as she turns to face Max.

"It's over," she announces. "I want you to leave Paris."

Max huffs, pushing himself off the wall. "Have it your way, Lucie. You'll regret this one day. I know you will." He lingers for a moment, his pained, scary stare making my stomach curl.

"She won't regret anything, Max," I say. I can't help myself.

Leo steps in, nodding toward the street. "You heard the lady."

Max gives Lucie one last shake of the head before rambling down the darkened cobblestone alley and letting himself into an old-fashioned black taxicab. It's only when the taillights finally disappear into the night that Lucie lets out a shaky breath.

I take her hand and squeeze it in mine, at once feeling the change in the air around us, the magnitude of what has just happened settling in. I'm not sure exactly how this scene played out the first time around when my grandma Ella was here, but I know that it must've ended with Lucie climbing into that car with Max, moving to New York soon after, and ending up in the faded newspaper clippings in my grandmother's photo album.

But tonight, as Lucie stands next to me, alive and well—albeit a little shaken up—I know without a doubt that the past has been forever altered. The chain of ill-fated events that led to Lucie's untimely death at the young age of twenty-three has been erased.

Leo and Jean-Philippe walk over to the lamppost, giving us some space to talk.

A tear streaks down Lucie's cheek as she turns to face me. "Thank you, Ella. Thank you for pulling me out of my Max haze. You know how he gets me all spun up, makes me not be able to see straight."

I wipe the tear away. "But *you* did it, Lucie. You stood up for yourself. And now you'll never be hurt by that man again. I'm so proud of you."

The slightest of smiles peppers her cheeks. "You're right. And you know what, it was scary, but it felt good."

I think of my past with Dave—or my future, rather—and for the first time, the thought of leaving him isn't so terrifying either.

"Still, Ella, I couldn't have done it without you by my side," she says. "You know that, don't you?"

I instinctively reach for Lucie, wrapping her up in a hug. I can almost feel the warmth of my grandmother's gaze shining down on us. Lucie is staying in Paris, and she's finished with Max forever, which means my grandma's one last regret has been taken care of. She can rest peacefully now.

But as Lucie pulls from my embrace and finds Jean-Philippe's welcoming arms waiting ever so patiently for her to return, I realize that I am still caught in this mysterious time warp, and I have no idea how I will make it back to my grandmother's bedside to share the good news.

Chapter Seven

The beady headlights of a beautiful 1920s-era automobile blind me momentarily, its humming engine making me remember where I am—and how implausible it is that I am even *here*.

Leo appears by my side, but I barely notice. I am still gawking at the classic car, at the old buildings that line this narrow little *rue,* at the glowing lampposts lighting the way for the drunk, merry Parisians strolling down the sidewalk in their vintage—well, modern—clothing. And I am wondering how in the hell this is possible. And how I will ever find my way back to my grandma Ella's modern-day apartment to say one last good-bye before it's too late.

"Lost again, Miss Ella?" Leo says, placing a hand on my shoulder.

I blink away my confusion as I turn to him. "No…no, I'm fine." A flush of warmth tickles my skin where Leo's hand lies, and as his intense blue gaze smiles back at me, I notice Lucie and Jean-Philippe have disappeared into the shadows.

"Thank you for helping Lucie," I say. "You didn't have to step in like you did."

Leo grins, taking a step closer. "I was happy to help,

although something tells me the two of you would've been just fine on your own. I've never seen a pair of ladies band together like that. You're not only stunning, you're a damn good friend, Miss Ella Carlyle."

My fingers find the hem of my dress, twirling it around like a young schoolgirl who's been bitten by a serious crush. And it feels absolutely wonderful. "Thanks, Leo. You're not so bad yourself."

"Listen, I think we've all probably had enough of this joint for one night. How about joining me for an open-air tour of Paris?"

"Open air?" I ask, but before he can answer me, a glossy maroon convertible chugs up to the curb and parks beside us.

The driver smiles, tipping his hat at Leo. *"Bonsoir,* Monsieur Knight."

Leo laughs, slapping his hand over the man's back. *"Bonsoir,* Guillaume. This is my new lady friend, Ella Carlyle," he says in French. "We're still waiting on two more."

Leo opens the door, and as I climb into the backseat, I feel about as excited as a little girl stepping onto a carnival ride. Leo hops in beside me, his eyes beaming, as Jean-Philippe and Lucie meander out onto the sidewalk hand in hand.

They squeeze into the front seat next to the driver, then Lucie flips her head of curly black hair and winks at me and Leo. "Thank you," she mouths before taking over the job of holding a bag of ice to Jean-Philippe's bruised face and kissing him gently on the cheek.

The two lovebirds snuggle up together as if the entire Max debacle never even happened, and as I watch them, I am filled with an overwhelming sense of hope. An event that must've gone so terribly wrong the first time around has been corrected. My presence here—and Leo's too—has altered this one night in history, which will change Lucie's and my grandma Ella's futures for the better.

Leo stretches a casual arm around my shoulders as he

calls up to the driver. "Let's give these lovely American ladies a tour of Paris, Guillaume!"

The driver tips his hat, then sets the old car into motion down the skinny alleyway. A warm night breeze tickles my cheeks, which feel as if they are on fire with each brush of Leo's hand on my shoulder. Our legs are pressed side by side in the velvety backseat, and as the wheels roll slowly over the bumpy cobblestones, Leo pulls me in closer.

I don't feel even an ounce of guilt over the fact that *technically* I have a boyfriend. And somewhere deep down, I realize that if I were never to see that boyfriend again, I wouldn't be too sad about it.

Pushing all thoughts of Dave and our grueling New York lifestyle out of my mind, I turn to Leo, to his shining blue eyes that reveal a zest for life I haven't felt for quite some time… that is, until tonight.

"What's going through that beautiful *tête* of yours, Miss Ella? Your wheels are spinning faster than this car," he says with a hearty laugh.

"I'm just thinking about how brave you were to handle Max like that. That punch you threw him was pretty impressive."

Leo shrugs and says quietly, "I grew up with a father who beat my ma, so I don't have a lot of patience for bullies. And I'm not afraid of them either. They're cowards, and that Max fella, well, he's as big of a coward as they come. Lucie will be better off never seeing his ugly mug again."

"You're right," I say with a laugh. "I think we'll *all* be better off."

"Besides, a city like Paris is too beautiful to be mucked up by the likes of him." Leo's dimple pops onto his left cheek as his grin widens. "Now you, on the other hand, Miss Ella Carlyle…I think the lights of Paris got a whole lot brighter the minute you stepped your lovely dancer feet into this town."

"Merci," I say, giving him a flirty bat of my eyelashes. God, when was the last time a man complimented me like this?

I couldn't care less that the handsome writer sitting beside me probably doesn't have more than a dime to his name. What matters is that Leo's not afraid to stand up for what he believes in, and most of all, he knows how to have fun, something I haven't done in *ages*.

Just as I find myself wishing there was a way to swap Dave for Leo, the car turns onto a lively tree lined boulevard. More of these shiny classic cars bumble past us, while Parisians and expats soak up the exciting nightlife, strolling from cafés to jazz clubs, smoking their long cigarettes, drinking wine, and flirting with the unmatchable charm of Paris on this summer night.

The women look impossibly glamorous in their glittery flapper dresses, and the men vying for their attention are young, handsome, and rowdy in their drunkenness. The sun must've set hours ago, yet this city is more awake and alive than I've ever seen it.

We cross through a busy intersection, and in the glow of the headlights, I spot the street signs on the corner of one of the elegant apartment buildings. We are at the intersection of boulevard Saint-Michel and boulevard Saint-Germain, only a few blocks away from the apartment building where my grandmother lives—in the twenty-first century.

Despite the humidity swimming through the city tonight, a chill slithers up my arms. The driver takes a right on boulevard Saint-Michel, leading us farther away from my grandma's future home. I wonder, if I were able to sneak into that same apartment tonight, would that be my ticket back?

Leo wraps his arm tighter around my shoulders, reminding me that I don't need a ticket back just yet.

"You know," he says. "Ever since I arrived in Paris a couple of months ago, I've found that my favorite time to explore the city is at night. I've never seen a city or its people come alive like this after dark. Have you ever seen anything like it, Ella?"

"No, I haven't," I say honestly. I want to tell Leo that I first fell in love with a different Paris, a Paris that is charming and gorgeous and still thriving almost a century in the future. But this old-world version of the city is leaving me speechless.

Finally, one word comes to mind, the only word I can think of to describe the enchanting sights before me.

"It's magical," I say, grinning up at Leo. "Paris at night is simply magical."

"I couldn't have said it better myself," he says as the car reaches the Seine and begins its journey across Pont Saint-Michel.

"Guillaume, would you mind letting me and Miss Ella out for a minute?" Leo says in French. "We'll catch up with you on the other side of the bridge."

"Mais bien sûr," Guillaume says, swerving the car to the right.

Leo opens the door, takes my hand, and leads me onto the sidewalk, where we are suddenly alone in the sparkling night. The deep-blue waters of the Seine glisten underneath the light of the full moon up above, which casts a glow on the two towers of Notre Dame Cathedral facing us.

Leo surprises me as he leans closer, his lips brushing over the tip of my ear. "There's something different in the air tonight. I felt it the minute I walked out my door. The city feels even more magical, even more mysterious than usual. Do you feel it, Ella?"

I swivel to face him, reveling in the warmth of his breath on my cheeks, of our noses touching as our bodies press together.

"Yes, I feel it."

Leo traces a finger along the neckline of my dress, then cups my cheek in his hand and smiles at me with his gorgeous eyes. "Whatever is in the air tonight, I reckon it's telling me to kiss you."

Leo lowers his lips to mine, and I tip up my chin to meet him halfway.

The bustling nightlife continues to move and swirl and unfold all around us, but as Leo kisses me atop this ancient bridge in the heart of Paris, it feels as if time stops.

With each brush of Leo's soft, warm lips, I feel something unraveling, something moving and changing inside of me. He pulls me in tighter as our kiss heats up the already blazing summer night, and a ripple of desire flows through my core, lighting a fire in me that no man has ever managed to light.

When our mouths finally part, the excitement and zest I suddenly feel for life—for *my* life—takes hold, and I am certain that after this thrilling night in Paris, after meeting Leo the writer from Saint Louis, I will never be the same.

By the way my handsome lover is gazing into my eyes with a passion and intensity I never experienced in my other life, I know he feels it too.

"You don't look lost anymore, Ella," he says, running his hands along the curves of my face and down over my bare shoulders. "In fact, you look like a woman who knows exactly what she wants."

"Oh, really?" I say. "And what is it that you think I want?"

"That sparkle in your eye is telling me you want to dance, Miss Ella. And luckily, I know just the place. Follow me." Leo wraps his hand around mine, that extra skip in his step leading us to the other side of the bridge, where Guillaume has pulled over to wait for us. As we climb into the backseat, Leo whispers something in Guillaume's ear, then taps Lucie and Jean-Philippe on the shoulders. "Two more stops tonight, folks. And I think you're going to love them."

Lucie lets out an excited squeal as Jean-Philippe kisses her on the cheek. "*On y va!*" she shouts. *Let's go!*

Bubbles of laughter erupt from the car, and our merriment

only grows as we take a left and trace a path up the Right Bank of the Seine, passing by the Pont Neuf, the majestic Palais du Louvre, and le Jardin des Tuileries. When we finally veer away from the river, I get my first glimpse of the 1927 version of the Champs-Élysées.

Old cars buzz and honk as they weave up and down the famous tree lined avenue. Without traffic lanes to keep the drivers in line, chaos ensues as far as I can see, all the way down to the grand Arc de Triomphe.

The monuments and many of the buildings I remember from modern-day Paris are all here, but the feel of the city is completely different. It's as if I've jumped inside a faded black-and-white postcard—except I'm seeing it all in color.

And it's the most vibrant, exciting picture I've ever seen.

We don't take the Champs, but instead head north through the city until we reach my favorite place in all of Paris—the Opéra Garnier. My fondest memories of my summers in Paris are of my grandma Ella taking me to see the ballet at this gorgeous opera house.

Tonight, with the lampposts lighting up the traffic circle, the pillars and golden statues that adorn the palace appear newer and shinier than I remember from my visits as a young girl many, many years in the future.

The driver pulls up to the opera steps, then turns and slips something into Leo's hands before tipping his hat to us.

"*Merci*, Guillaume," Leo says, tucking what looks like a set of keys into his pocket. Then he hops out of the car and motions for us to follow.

"Are we going—?"

"Patience, Miss Ella. You'll see." Leo taps Guillaume on the shoulder. "See you in an hour?" he says in French.

Guillaume nods, then pulls away from the curb, leaving me, Lucie, and Jean-Philippe staring up at the regal opera house.

Leo runs up the stairs ahead of us. "Well, come on!" he calls out. "We don't have long."

The three of us race up the steps after him like a group of jubilant, rebellious teenagers. Jean-Philippe's face is still a mess from the beat-down earlier, but he doesn't seem to care as he holds Lucie's hand and laughs with her all the way up the stairs.

When we reach the top, Leo takes my hand and leads us around the side of the theater to a back entrance. He takes a quick peek around to make sure no one is watching, then pulls out the keys and unlocks the door.

"Hurry!" he whispers, ushering us in.

Inside, we take off down a dark hallway that eventually opens up into what appears to be the backstage area.

As we try to stave off the giggles, Leo stops running, bringing a finger to his lips. "Okay, stay here, and I'll be right back."

Lucie grabs my hand. "Where did you get this guy, Ella?" she whispers. "I love him!"

I squeeze her hand, my smile lighting up in the darkness.

A few seconds later, Leo returns. "The coast is clear. Follow me."

We weave around a tall curtain, then Leo feels around on the wall and begins hitting rows upon rows of switches.

Bright white lights flicker on, startling me as they illuminate the expansive stage beyond the wings. Lucie lets out an excited yelp as the three of us walk out onto the stage and take in the view.

A sea of red velvet seats stretches out before us, and rows of golden balconies climb all the way to the ceiling, which holds an impressive—and *massive*—bronze-and-crystal chandelier. I notice that the colorful Chagall painting that swirls across the ceiling of the modern-day opera house hasn't yet been painted. But the missing painting doesn't steal a single ounce of glory from this breathtaking theater.

A lively jazz tune filters out from the wings, and just as Jean-Philippe and Lucie begin bopping around the stage hand in hand, Leo appears by my side.

His grin lights up brighter than the chandelier as he gestures to our surroundings. "What do you think?"

My heart swells with emotion as I turn to Leo in utter amazement. "It's incredible. How did you pull this off?"

"My friend Guillaume works backstage here. I did him a pretty big favor a few weeks back, and I told the fellow I didn't want anything in return, but he insisted on being my chauffeur for the night." Leo takes a purposeful step toward me. "And as luck would have it, tonight was the night I met a beautiful ballerina. I thought you might like to come to the Palais Garnier when we could have the whole place to ourselves."

Suddenly Leo sweeps me into his arms and dips me backward until my head almost touches the floor. His lips cover mine, and once again, I feel the tightness that has been lodged in my chest for years now releasing.

After his toe-curling kiss, he swings me back up, twirls me around, and pulls me tightly into his chest.

"Pretty swell, isn't it?" he says.

"Swell doesn't even begin to describe this night with you, Leo," I answer. "It's the best night I've had in a long time."

"And it's not even halfway over," he says, wrapping his hands around mine and breaking into the Charleston.

We swing our legs and arms out to the sides, and this time, I'm lighter on my feet, more confident with the moves, and having the absolute time of my life.

"I know we've only just met," Leo says in between kicks, "but this song reminds me of you, Ella. That's why I picked it. Do you know this one?"

The familiar female voice in the old twenties tune makes me think of a record my grandma used to play, and after I listen for a few moments, I've got it.

"Josephine Baker?"

Leo winks. "The one and only. I saw her perform this song live last month. It's called 'Then I'll Be Happy.' Have you seen her in Paris yet?"

"No, but I would love to," I say, thinking about how exciting it would be to stay here and enjoy the glittery Jazz Age with Leo dancing by my side.

"Well, my pretty lady, we'll have to arrange it."

Leo spins me around in fast, tight circles, and my feet move effortlessly along with the beat. In fact, this whole night with Leo feels effortless, like a dream—the sweetest dream I've ever had.

Lucie and Jean-Philippe hop up beside us, beaming from ear to ear as they dance off the earlier stress from the fight and find comfort in each other's arms.

After almost an hour of nonstop dancing, laughing, and occasional sipping from Jean-Philippe's flask, which he so generously passes around, the music ends, and it's time to go.

I hesitate, taking one more look around the brilliant theater, realizing that no one, in all my life, has ever done something so spontaneous, so thrilling, so romantic as what Leo has done for me tonight.

And if I go back to Dave, to the limiting life I've created in New York, I am certain that nothing this magical will ever happen again.

I want nothing more than to stay in Jazz-Age Paris with this brilliant man by my side. I want to dance with him all night, share a strong French coffee with him in the morning, and see where our thrilling encounter might lead.

But my clock is ticking. And in the end, I know I'll have to leave him.

Leo takes my face in his hands. "Don't cry, Ella. The night isn't over yet."

"It's just so beautiful," I say, swallowing the knot in my throat. "Thank you, Leo. Thank you for giving me this gift."

He kisses me once more underneath the bright stage lights, then whispers in my ear, "We still have one more stop on our tour of Paris. I think you're going to love this one."

"I have no doubt I will."

What I also don't doubt is that dawn is quickly approaching, and if my grandma was right, I don't have much time left.

Chapter Eight

*L*ucie has fallen asleep on Jean-Philippe's shoulder by the time we reach our last stop, but I am more awake than ever.

I desperately need to make it back to my grandma before it's too late, but my heart is breaking over the thought of leaving Leo behind.

Guillaume parks on a darkened street where only an occasional car chugs past.

Leo hops out of the car, then reaches for my hand.

"Should we wake them up?" I whisper, nodding to the two lovebirds sleeping in the front seat.

"Nah, let 'em sleep," Leo says as I slip my hand into his outstretched one and slide out of the car.

Only a few dim lampposts light the way as we take off down the empty sidewalk. "Where are we?" I ask.

Leo kisses me on the cheek, setting those butterflies in motion again. "You'll see," he says.

A few moments later, we emerge to an opening beyond the trees lining the sidewalk, and there, across the calm waters of the Seine, stands the Eiffel Tower. Dazzling white lights climb up the length of the tower, spelling out the word

Citroën, which I recognize as a popular brand of French cars. Each letter appears like a bold, glowing brushstroke from a giant paintbrush.

"Monsieur Citroën sure does know how to advertise, huh?" Leo says, nodding up at the impressive tower. "I think the tower would look so much nicer at night with lights that sparkle, that shine without any words or advertisements."

I smile, thinking of the sparkling lights that will adorn the tower in the future—no words, no advertisements, just as Leo says.

"I agree," I say. "It's too beautiful to be used as a billboard. But I have to say, it's still breathtaking."

Leo turns to me. "That it is, sweetheart. Now follow me. There's one last thing I want to show you."

We turn away from the tower and head toward a small circle lit up by the glow of the streetlamps. In the center of the circle, there is a lovely carousel—a carousel I remember. My grandma used to take me here often when I was little.

Leo squeezes my hand, and we run up to the beautifully crafted but dark merry-go-round. "Climb aboard, Miss Ella!" he says as he searches for the switch.

"Are we allowed to do this?"

Leo laughs. "Of course not. That's what makes it so fun. Now climb aboard!"

I hop up onto the platform and swing my leg over the prettiest horse I can find. Just as the carousel lights up and starts to spin, Leo saddles up beside me.

An old tune flitters through the night as our horses move up and down, side by side, across the river from the sparkling Eiffel Tower. Leo's captivating grin and his contagious laughter are the icing on the cake for this perfect, magical moment.

Our hands instinctively reach for one another between the moving horses and Leo sizes me up, casting a perplexed gaze in my direction.

"What is it?" I ask.

"You're different from the other girls, you know that, Ella? You've got something mysterious hiding behind those beautiful blue eyes of yours," Leo says. "Like you're keeping a secret. *A big one.*"

I wish I could tell Leo my big secret, but how would he ever believe me? Like Lucie, he'd probably think I'd had too much to drink. That or he'd think I was clinically insane.

"What's your secret, Ella? If you tell me yours, I'll tell you mine."

"Oh, you have a secret too, do you?" I say, flashing him a flirty smile. "That's a pretty compelling offer."

"All right, then, what do you say?"

I nod. "I'm in. But only if you go first."

The carousel gains in speed, the music picking up in tempo as a warm breeze blows against my cheeks, which are already hot underneath Leo's intense gaze.

"Here goes," he says. "I haven't written a story in over a year. That's why I moved to Paris. I was hoping something would strike me here—that strolling along these cobblestone streets, drinking wine at cafés, listening to the beautiful language, and watching artists paint the city would inspire me…would give me something real, something true to write about. And this city *has* inspired me, but I still haven't come up with a good story idea…until tonight."

I raise a brow at him. "Really? You have an idea now?"

He nods, his eyes sparkling with excitement. "I do. I'm going to write a story about an American girl—a ballet dancer—who comes to Paris and meets a boy—a writer, perhaps—in a jazz club. And I'm going to write about the one magical night they spend together in the most romantic city in the world."

"I love it," I say, squeezing Leo's hand as our horses continue to trot side by side. "It's perfect."

"It just might be, but that all depends on the ending." Leo flashes me a mischievous look.

"And how do you want the story to end?" I ask, trying to suppress the sinking feeling that grips my heart as I glimpse a swirl of pink and purple clouds lighting up the eastern sky.

Leo leans toward me until his lips are an inch from mine. "That's just it, Ella Carlyle. I don't want our story to end."

"I don't want it to end either," I tell him, knowing I've never meant anything more in my entire life.

The minute our lips meet, the carousel spins faster. But even as a gust of hot summer air blows at our cheeks and the music picks up to a heart-quickening speed, we don't break our kiss.

The wind swoops in, blowing my hair back until I hear something clatter on the carousel floor. But I barely notice. I am lost in a trance as Leo holds me in the heat of his kiss.

Suddenly it feels as if my feet have landed on solid ground, and they are moving—spinning in frantic, fast circles. A harsh breeze replaces the warmth of Leo's lips on mine, and in a panic, I open my eyes.

Dizzily, I stumble into a full-length mirror. Grabbing onto the sides of the glass to steady myself, I blink a few times, willing Leo's face, his sweet eyes, his full head of dusty-blond hair to reappear.

But all I find is my bewildered face reflected back at me, my short blonde hair all windblown and a gap in my headpiece where the sparkly red brooch was pinned only moments ago.

The clatter on the carousel floor. It was the brooch.

I turn around, scanning my surroundings—but Leo is gone.

Instead, I find my grandmother lying in the center of her four-poster bed, struggling to breathe.

I rush to her side, scooping up her hands and kissing her on the forehead.

"I'm back," I whisper softly in her ear. "It's me, little Ella."

Her chest rises slowly as she squeezes my hand. "Ella," she says as the corners of her lips turn upward.

Is she smiling?

"Yes, it's me," I say.

She opens her eyes, and despite the shallow breaths that pass through her lips, she breaks into a full-on grin. "Lucie," she says. "You did it. You saved her."

Suddenly, a vivid memory of me and my grandma riding our matching bicycles through the hilly streets of Montmartre rushes into my mind. Except the memory is different now—a third person is riding alongside us.

Lucie.

"She didn't leave Paris with Max," I say aloud. "Lucie lived. But how did you know I could go back in time? How did you know I would be able to save her?"

"There's a bit of magic in that sparkly red brooch, my dear," she whispers. "I may have used it once or twice myself…but I couldn't let you have it until you were ready."

"But I lost the brooch. It fell off at the end of the night, and I—" I stop, not wanting to relive the heart-wrenching moment when Leo's lips left mine.

"Shhh," she soothes. "It served its purpose, now didn't it?" Tears line my grandma's eyes as she blinks up at me. "Lucie lived, and so will you, Ella. That is my last wish. That you live the life you've always dreamed of. The life only you can create. Settle for nothing less, my dear Ella. Promise me that."

Tucking a strand of her thin silvery hair behind her ear, I smile down at this amazing woman who has given me the most incredible gift. "I promise." Tears stream down my cheeks now as I hold her in my arms. "Thank you, Grandma Ella. Thank you so much."

That beautiful smile on her face stays as she closes her

eyes. And as her chest rises and falls with each slowing breath, a whisper escapes her lips.

"Our favorite bookstore," she says. "Go there. Find the book."

But before I can ask her which book she is talking about, her breath catches in her throat, her eyelashes fluttering ever so slightly, and I find myself praying for a miracle.

Please stay with me for just a few more moments. Please, Grandma. Don't go.

By the way her breath is slowing, her chest barely rising now, I know that this is it.

"I love you, Grandma Ella. I will always love you," I tell her through my tears.

The corners of her mouth turn up into a beautiful, heart-breaking smile as she takes in one final breath.

My dear grandma Ella is gone.

Chapter Nine

"*Voilà*, mademoiselle," the Parisian cabdriver says as he sets my suitcase onto the sidewalk and admires the charming apartment building before us.

"An apartment on boulevard Saint-Germain...*pas mal*." he says, giving me a nod. *Not bad.*

I smile as I hand him a stack of euros. "Not bad at all," I say, turning toward my new home. "*Merci*, monsieur," I call as he climbs into the driver's seat and joins the herds of tiny French cars zooming up and down the bustling boulevard.

The familiar aroma of freshly baked baguettes, buttery croissants, and chocolate-filled pastries drifts out from the *boulangerie* at the corner—the same *boulangerie* my grandma used to take me to during my summers in Paris, and the one I will be visiting quite frequently from this day forward... because I live here now.

I almost have to pinch myself as I walk up to the front door and punch in the code.

This isn't a dream, I remind myself. I've actually moved to Paris.

When my grandma asked for me to be with her in those final moments, she left me with the two most important gifts of my life—one unforgettable night in Paris in the 1920s *and* her elegant apartment on boulevard Saint-Germain.

She must've known I would need them both.

After she passed, I was devastated over her loss and over losing Leo, but I didn't waste a single moment in my efforts to fulfill the promise I had made to her, the promise that I would live. *Truly live.*

Well…I *may* have made myself sick from the hours I spent spinning in front of her mirror, dressed in her red flapper dress, trying to twirl my way back to the past—and more specifically, to Leo.

But when I finally came to terms with the reality that I'd been given one night, and one night only, I bucked up and made a new life plan for myself.

That plan involved quitting my coveted associate position at the new law firm where I'd only just begun working, and harnessing the courage to break up with Dave and move out of our loveless New York City apartment. The breakup wasn't pretty—Dave ranted and raved like a two-year-old who needed a nap, but after my night with Lucie, I wasn't afraid of him or his empty threats any longer. I'd made my decision, and nothing he could've said or done would've stopped me.

When I finally left, the cherry on top of it all was making the permanent move to Paris.

The past two months have been a whirlwind—and not an easy whirlwind, at that—but none of that matters now that I am here.

Now that I am home.

It's my first night back in Paris, and as I walk alone down the *quai* of the Seine, I remember my words to Leo.

"Paris at night is simply magical."

With the French language twirling past me, the smell of

delicious French cuisine floating out from sidewalk cafés, and the full moon shining brightly overhead, I realize that tonight, of all nights, that statement has never been more true.

Veering away from the banks of the Seine, I cross over rue du Petit Pont and walk swiftly, nearly breaking into a jog, until I come upon the quaint English bookstore that has adorned Paris's Left Bank for years, the bookstore that holds so many fond memories from my summers in Paris with Grandma Ella—Shakespeare and Company.

Inside, as I take in the rows upon rows of old books jammed into this historical landmark, I am both over-whelmed and excited.

I'm not here to browse. I'm here to find one specific book.

As I run my fingers over the leathery spines and trace my way to the back of the store, I can feel the spark in the air.

I know it's here.

The smell of worn pages accompanies me as I scan the shelves for what feels like hours. I don't lose my patience though. After all, if I don't find the book tonight, I will keep searching tomorrow and the day after, and the day after that, because the book I'm looking for—the book my grandma told me to find just before she took her last breath—is the only possible connection I have left to the fun-loving, romantic young writer who I met on a hot summer night in Paris in 1927.

The writer I cannot stop thinking about. The man I would give anything to see again, even if it were only for one more night.

I have no idea what happened to Leo after I disappeared from the carousel. After my grandma passed, I searched her old photo albums for Leo's charming smile, for that hand-some face, but I never found it. There were photos of my grandma and her best friend Lucie all the way up until Lucie's death at the ripe old age of ninety-five—which proves that my unbelievable time-travel experience was not just a dream, that I did in fact help to save Lucie's life and change the course of history—but as for Leo, he wasn't in those albums.

Still, if that brief but magical night we spent together meant even half as much to him as it meant to me—and I'm certain it did—then I know he would've written about it.

And so, on this first night back in Paris, I tirelessly comb the shelves of Shakespeare and Company for a book written by Leo Knight. It is only when the storekeeper announces closing time that I feel my shoulders slump, my heart ache.

Just as I am turning to leave, resolving to start a new search tomorrow, I take one more quick look over the shelves in front of me, and finally, something catches my eye.

I am so jet-lagged from my journey across the ocean that I'm not sure if I'm reading the faded print correctly, but when I remove the thin book that has been crammed into the corner of the shelf, there is no mistaking the name printed on the old, weathered spine.

L. Knight

The front cover is so faded that I can't read the title, but when I flip open the book, there it is.

One Magical Night in Paris
by L. Knight

"I'm sorry, mademoiselle, but we're closing now," the storekeeper says over my shoulder. "Would you like to buy that?"

I turn to him, unable to hide the tears that gloss over my eyes. "Yes, I would," I say quietly, clutching the book to my heart.

After I pay, I keep Leo's book, his story of our night together, pressed closely to my chest until I find a quiet little café on the Left Bank, only steps away from where the jazz club had been that night.

With my strong French coffee in hand, I open Leo's book and dive into its pages, enraptured by the beautiful words he wrote for me so many years ago. He tells the story of one hot Parisian night in June of 1927 when a young writer from Saint Louis meets an American ballerina in a jazz club and they spend a magical night together in the City of Light.

Reading Leo's description of the most enchanting night of my life is an emotional and overwhelming experience. He explains that he knew right from the start, from the moment he first laid eyes on me, that I wasn't like the other girls. He noticed that I talked differently, held myself differently than the other women—almost as if I were from a different era altogether.

All throughout the evening, he had a feeling that our time together was limited. Which was why he didn't want to waste a single moment.

As I near the final pages of the story, I am overcome with love for Leo, with nostalgia for the moments we spent together, and with gratitude for his zest for life —which, in addition to my grandmother's urgent message, inspired me to change my own life for the better.

But most of all, I am saddened, broken over the fact that I will never again see his smiling face, hear his excited voice, or kiss those sweet lips.

Just before the café is about to close, I turn to the very last page. A handwritten note is scrawled across the inside of the back cover, and as I read the words Leo wrote just for me, a new emotion fills my heart—*hope*.

My beautiful Ella,
I don't know where you've gone, or where you came from,
but if ever you read the words on this page (or on one of the
many pages from this same book that I have placed in just

about every bookstore in Paris), know that I left my heart
with you on that carousel, and until I see your pretty face
again, that is where it will stay.
Forever yours,
Leo

Closing the book, I toss a few euros onto the table and dash out of the café to catch a cab.

I know that what I'm about to do defies all logic, but in this new life of mine, there is no room for logic.

There is only room for love.

By the time I reach the carousel, the tourists have gone home, and the normally buzzing streets are empty.

With Leo's book still clutched tightly to my heart, I climb the steps to the carousel platform, running a hand over the delicately painted horses until I find the one I'm looking for.

Swinging my leg over the saddle of the same horse I rode next to Leo only two months—but almost a century—ago, I gaze out at the Eiffel Tower, marveling at the way the full moon illuminates the top and casts a shimmer on the deep-blue waters of the Seine.

A late summer breeze flutters past my cheeks, and just as I am closing my eyes, the carousel starts to spin. A dated jazz tune filters out of the speakers as the merry-go-round picks up speed and twirls me in circles. I keep my eyes closed as I remember the exhilaration I felt when Leo took my hand, when he kissed me on this very carousel.

Suddenly, I picture his face. I see his bright-blue eyes as clear as day, as if they are shining right in front of me.

"Why, Miss Ella, I do believe you lost this."

It's his voice…Leo's voice.

But it can't be.

My eyes pop open, and there beside me stands Leo, grinning his charming, adorable, knee-weakening grin.

He holds up the sparkly red brooch and clips it to my hair before cupping my face in his palms.

"Leo, you're here! You're really here." I say, noticing the change in the air around us, the energy, the excitement that takes hold of me the minute his skin touches mine.

He laughs. "I know. I can't quite believe it myself."

"How?" I ask. "How did you get here?"

"After I wrote the book, which I see you found," he pauses, nodding toward the old story in my lap, "I came back to this carousel every night, hoping I would find you. Hoping it would lead me to you somehow. And when I arrived here tonight, I had an inkling to look around, see if you left anything behind. And that's when I found this beautiful stone, the one you were wearing in your hair that night." He traces a finger over the shiny brooch, then runs his hand over my bare shoulder.

"The minute I picked it up, the carousel started spinning, and suddenly, here I was…and here *you* are, looking as beautiful as ever."

Leo laces his hands through my hair and pulls me in for a kiss. A spark of electricity soars through my entire body at the feel of his lips on mine. When our mouths part and I see that he is still standing here in the flesh and blood, relief floods through me.

"Are you here to stay?" I ask.

Leo's eyes light up. "When I said I didn't want our story to end, I meant it, Ella Carlyle."

"Good, because I don't want it to end either."

Leo lifts me off the horse and carries me off the carousel and into the warm night, the two of us laughing all the way. Across the river, a brilliant show of sparkling lights illuminates the Eiffel Tower, and Leo stops walking, staring up in amazement.

"Ella?" he says, still holding me in his arms.

"Yes, Leo?"

"It's not 1927 in Paris anymore, is it?"

I jump from his arms, landing on my feet right in front of him. "No, it's not," I say, taking his hand. "But don't worry, I'll show you around. A lot has changed since we last saw each other."

Leo shrugs as a hearty laugh escapes his lips. "So this was your big secret, eh? Well, this was quite a secret, Miss Ella… and *you* are quite the lady."

Leo leans in for one more smoldering kiss before we take off through the winding streets of Paris, the first of *many* unforgettable nights we will spend together in this magical City of Light.

A Note from Juliette

Thank you so much for reading *One Night in Paris*. I hope you enjoyed Ella's magical journey through the City of Light, and I am excited to tell you there will be more to come!

If you would like to leave an honest review for *One Night in Paris* on the site where you purchased the book, I would appreciate it so much. Reviews are so incredibly helpful for authors, and I have been touched by the lovely reviews many of you have left for my books over the years.

If you loved Ella's French adventures and would like to continue your magical time travel journey through Paris, you can save on the next two books in the series by reading the newly released omnibus edition: *The City of Light Series: Books 1-3*.

Much like Ella, I fell in love with Paris the minute I stepped foot onto its lovely cobblestone streets, and I have been writing books based in this beautiful city ever since. Read on for descriptions of all of my novels, excerpts of Books 2 and 3 in my *City of Light Series*, and to find out how you can receive three of my bestselling books for *free!*

Juliette Sobanet's Free Starter Library

One of my favorite parts about being a writer is building a relationship with my amazing readers! I love hearing from you, and I also love letting you know what's going on in my world. Occasionally I send out brief newsletters with details on my new releases and special offers just for you. If you'd like to be the first to find out about my new releases and receive your *free* Juliette Sobanet Starter Library, I'll send you:

1. A free copy of the award-winning first novel in my *City of Love* series: *Sleeping with Paris.*
2. A free copy of the bestselling novella in my *City of Light* series: *One Night in Paris.*
3. A free copy of the first spicy novella in my *City Girls* series: *Confessions of a City Girl: Los Angeles.*

To receive your free ebooks, simply head over to my website at *www.juliettesobanet.com* and sign up for my newsletter. I'll be thrilled to send them to you!

Dancing with Paris Excerpt

CITY OF LIGHT BOOK 2

Dancing with Paris

CHAPTER ONE

"Claudia, what do I always tell you? Salsa comes from the hips! Now, *move*!"

My face flamed as Kosta, my Serbian-born salsa instructor, squared himself in front of me, then grabbed my hips and tried to emulate the smooth gyrations that were coming from his own. When I snuck a glimpse of myself in the mirror, I decided I looked more like a swollen purple balloon jiggling atop of a pair of stilts than the Latin dance goddess Kosta expected.

And of all nights, tonight was *not* the night to look like a swollen *anything*.

But I wouldn't let the growing baby bump hiding underneath my loose violet tank stop me from telling Édouard the truth. Tonight was my last chance.

If only he would get here.

I glanced at the clock as my feet stumbled to keep up with the rapid Latin beat booming through my grandmother's San Diego dance studio.

It was already seven thirty. He'd never been this late before.

Kosta grabbed my chin and swiveled my face back to his.

"He'll be here, Miss Claudia. And in the meantime, you need to focus. Focus on the movements. On the hips. On the *sex*. Like I always teach you." Kosta twirled me around, then pulled me back into his chest as he flipped his full head of wavy brown hair over to one side. "After all, what do you think Édouard is going to want to do with you tonight once you make your confession?"

I pulled away from Kosta's grasp and shot him a scowl. "The point of telling Édouard the truth about me being pregnant is not to get him into bed."

Kosta raised one perfectly plucked eyebrow, his hands on his bony hips. "What? A thirty-five-year-old woman cannot make the sex just because she is pregnant? If sex is not the point, Miss Claudia, then what is?"

Over the past five years that I'd been taking lessons at my grandma Martine's dance studio, Kosta *and* his inappropriately tight black pants had become like family to me. And just like family, sometimes I wanted to smack him.

"The *point* is that for the past three months, I've told Édouard everything about myself, *except* for the most important thing of all: that I'm pregnant. And that I'm going to be a single mother. Because I was too…I was too—"

"Cowardly? Scared?"

I sighed. "Yes. Thank you for that. But really, when Édouard and I first became dance partners, what was I going to do? Tell him that I just found out I'm pregnant and that the father of the baby turned out to be a married asshole who wants nothing to do with his child?"

Kosta shrugged, his twenty-five-year-old eyes revealing their naivety. "Why not?"

"Édouard didn't even know me. You can't blurt out that kind of humiliating information to a perfect stranger. *Especially* not to a handsome, famous actor like Édouard Marceau. But then once we got to know each other more and started going out together after class, and I…I started falling for him,

I just never found the right time to tell him. I mean, seriously, what man would want to date a woman who's about to have some other man's baby?"

Kosta pulled at my loose purple tank. "Well, you can't hide behind these poofy tops forever."

"Besides the fact that I'm just starting to show, you know it's Édouard's last night here before he leaves for Brazil for three months to shoot his next film, and if I don't tell him now—"

"You will always wonder, could I have gotten that sexy French actor into my bed? Even with a pregnant belly that will soon look like a small basketball?"

This time I did smack Kosta. Once on the right arm. And again on the left.

"I am sorry, Miss Claudia. You know, I kid. You are beautiful. And while Édouard is a little too *French* for my taste, he is clearly a much better man than Ian, that bag of scum. Plus, I have never seen you dance better than you do with Édouard. There is a…how do you say in English? An energy? Yes, an energy between the two of you. It is intense. It is sexy. I have never seen anything like it."

The flush on my cheeks crept down to my neck. "Let's not get carried away," I said to Kosta, although as I searched the studio to make sure Édouard hadn't walked in unnoticed, I knew Kosta was right. I felt that energy, that inexplicable connection. I'd felt it the moment Édouard had first walked into the dance studio three months ago.

But now, as I waited for him to make that same entrance, the only person I spotted was my elegant grandmother, practicing a waltz with one of the many older men who frequented the popular studio just to have the opportunity to dance with the infamous Martine Porter. Her soft, springy red curls coupled with her dazzling smile and her ability to tear up a dance floor still drew them in from miles away.

I clearly hadn't inherited my grandmother's man-magnet skills.

I pulled away from Kosta, the clock above the open window now reading a quarter till eight, my heart sinking into my chest.

Édouard wasn't coming.

"Kosta, I think I'd better call it a night. It's been a long day." I turned from him as I blinked away the warm tears that had sprung to my eyes.

Damn hormones.

I walked over to the bench on the far side of the studio, and my gaze immediately caught the scarlet-red journal sticking out of my purse. I couldn't help but open it up and pull out the small black-and-white sonogram picture I'd tucked inside after my doctor's appointment earlier that day.

As I gazed down at the cute little blob that was my baby's head, a gush of warmth laced with a twinge of sadness rushed through me.

"Looks like it's just going to be me and you, baby girl," I whispered as I patted my belly then tucked the photo back into my journal. But just as I was closing the book, the *other* picture I kept inside those worn pages slipped into my hands.

It was a photo of me as an innocent-faced little girl, sitting on my father's lap, smiling at him as if he were the only man on earth worthy of my love.

And completely oblivious to the fact that he would be taken from me only a year later.

I shook off the familiar feeling of guilt that threatened to engulf me as I gazed into my dad's eyes, an endless sea of blue that mirrored my own. I wondered, if he were here now, would he be disappointed in me?

What would he think of the fact that I made my living as a marriage and family therapist, counseling *others* on how to keep their families together, yet somehow here I was—thirty-five, pregnant, and single? *And* on the night I was finally going to open up to the man I truly cared about, he wasn't even going to show.

If I couldn't keep a man around, would I really be enough for my little girl?

Tucking the old photograph of me and my father back into my journal, I blew a strand of my long, chestnut-brown hair out of my eyes and plopped down on the bench, exasperated. But just as I was bending over to take off my glittery red heels, a sweet, rose-scented perfume wafted my way.

I closed my eyes and inhaled the scent, feeling a strange calm momentarily wash over me. My shoulders relaxed, the knot in my chest loosened, and when I opened my eyes, I found a striking older woman sitting next to me. She looked older than my grandmother and not nearly as glamorous. But as her silvery hair glistened underneath the bright lights of the dance studio and her oval-shaped violet eyes sparkled back at me, I felt as if I knew her somehow.

"Did you lose this?" she asked, stretching her weathered hand in my direction.

I gazed down to find my grandmother's heart-shaped ruby-red pendant dangling from the woman's fingers.

"That's my grandmother's favorite necklace. It must've slipped off her somehow. She'll be so happy you found it."

A mischievous gleam flashed in the woman's eyes as she unhooked the clasp on the silver chain. "It looks like your grandmother is busy over there, so why don't you wear the necklace tonight? The ruby will bring out that gorgeous sparkle in your blue eyes."

My cheeks flushed as I gazed down at the vintage neck-lace, which I'd never once seen my grandmother take off. The gorgeous stone twinkled in the old woman's hands, and before I could say no, she had already reached behind me and fastened the silver chain around my neck. She arranged the sparkling ruby heart in the center of my chest then beamed back at me with a warm, knowing smile.

"Just like I remembered. Stunning."

"I'm sorry. Have we met?" I ran my hand instinctively over the finely cut stone. But when a sharp spark flashed under my fingertips, I jumped in my seat.

"What the heck?" I said, shaking my hand out as the jolt of electricity sizzled underneath my skin.

The old woman chuckled, then raised a silvery brow. "Sometimes all it takes is a little jewelry to bring the spark back to your life, no?"

A bubble of nervous laughter escaped from my lips as I bent over again to slip off my heels. "No, I think this is a case of pregnancy exhaustion paired with mild delirium. Thank you for finding the necklace, though. I know my grandma will really appreciate it."

The old woman laid her warm hand on my arm. "I wouldn't take your dancing shoes off quite yet, if I were you," she said with a wink before lifting her striking eyes toward the front of the studio.

I opened my mouth to ask her what she was talking about, but when I followed her gaze, my breath caught in my lungs and refused to exhale.

With his head of jet-black unruly hair, his smoky-gray eyes, and his rugged five o'clock shadow, Édouard bounded across the shiny hardwood floors straight toward me.

"Breathe," came the old woman's soothing voice. "Just breathe."

I finally puffed out my bated breath and glanced quickly to my left, but the silver-haired woman was gone. All that remained was the lingering scent of roses and the distinct feeling of Édouard Marceau's gaze piercing through the cool, salty air in the beachside studio and straight into my soul.

Where had the woman gone? And why did I feel as if I'd met her before?

And why on earth was my hand still tingling?

When I lifted my eyes back up, I found Édouard standing over me, his breath heavy and his gaze serious.

"Dance with me, Claudia." He stretched out his hand, the determined look in his eyes telling me he wasn't going to take no for an answer.

I rested my hand inside Édouard's; more tiny sparks ignited under my skin at the mere feel of his touch. Hope rose in my chest as he swept me onto the dance floor.

"I hope you didn't think I wasn't coming," Édouard whispered in my ear as we fell into the natural rhythm we'd had since that first night he'd asked me to dance.

As our feet and hips swayed in perfect unison to the sultry beat of the salsa music lacing through the air, and my baby filled the tiny gap between us, I couldn't get a single word past my lips.

He'd shown up.

And before he walked back out those doors tonight, I had to tell him the truth.

Édouard wrapped his arm around my waist and pulled me closer to him, his grip tighter, more urgent than the other nights. As if there wasn't a moment to lose.

His deep voice cut through the music before I had a chance to speak. "I've been wanting to tell you since the first night we met…you're a stunning dancer, Claudia."

A blazing heat fanned over my cheeks as I focused on keeping my balance. "You're not so bad yourself."

He gave me his first sultry grin of the evening. "*Merci.* I must make a confession to you, though. These are not the only dance lessons I have ever taken."

"Oh?"

"When I was growing up in Paris, it was my mother who taught me how to dance. You see, in the fifties, she was a dancer near the famous Latin Quarter of Paris."

"Really? I can't believe you've never mentioned that." *God, I was one to talk.* "My grandmother spent some time dancing in Paris when she was younger too. She never talks about it much, but I can only imagine how glamorous it must've been. I've never even been to Paris."

"Ah, *Paris*. There is nowhere in the world like it," he said. "When you leave your apartment in the morning, you smell fresh *croissants, le café, et le chocolat*. You see couples kissing on the streets, not caring who might be watching. You sit for hours at cafés with your friends and drink wine and talk about nothing and everything." Édouard blinked away the wistfulness in his gaze, then twirled me around and pulled me tightly into his chest. "You must go someday. I am sure you would adore Paris."

Suddenly, a scene of a busy Parisian boulevard packed with old cars and lively French cafés flittered through my mind. I could almost feel the soles of my shoes on the rough cobblestones; hear the French chatter swirling around my head; and smell the coffee, the buttery croissants, and the chocolate, just as Édouard had said. It felt so strangely familiar, as if I'd actually been there.

But then Édouard's hips shifted against mine, jarring me back to the present, erasing the vivid scene from my confused head.

I told myself that the vibrant picture of Paris I'd just envisioned must've been from all of the old films I'd watched with my grandmother.

But it felt so real.

Shaking off the bizarre notion that something strange was happening, I told myself I was simply nervous. I focused on Édouard's handsome face, his hands around my waist. It was time to come clean.

But as the salsa tune came to an abrupt halt and a dark, seductive tango took its place, for some reason, in my jumbled mind, the sexy beat rang a bell of recognition.

Focus, Claudia. Focus.

I cleared my throat over the loud music and focused on

Édouard's smoky-gray eyes. "Édouard, there's something I need to—"

"Shhh," he whispered as he leaned closer to me, his lips brushing softly over my ear, his hot breath warming my already flaming skin. "Just for tonight—for our last night— let's forget about everything else that is going on in our lives. Just dance with me."

Édouard's firm shoulders locked into place, his strong arms enveloping me as he led me around the dance floor. All words escaped my lips once more, and as his silent gaze cut through me, I wondered what was going on in *his* life that he wanted to forget. Perhaps whatever it was had made him late tonight.

Before I could ask, a gust of bitter cold air swept through the dance studio as two teenage girls bounced through the front door. A chill rolled down my spine as I wondered how the temperature had dropped so fast. December in San Diego had *never* felt this icy.

My eyes stayed on those girls and their long blonde pony-tails, which bobbed as they tossed their purses onto the bench and sat down to change into their heels. But when one of their designer bags toppled over, a magazine slid out and skidded to a stop right next to our feet.

I peered down at the glossy cover of the latest *People* magazine, and my heart stopped.

Édouard's charming smile beamed up at me, and next to him stood a young, rail-thin French actress named Solange Raspail, one hand on her emaciated hip, the other draped loosely through Édouard's arm.

And above her chilly smile, I read the word *engaged.*

Édouard snatched the magazine up off the floor before I could reach it then marched it over to the girls. "I believe you dropped this," he snapped at them before tossing the maga-zine onto the bench and striding back over to me, a flare of anger present in his gaze.

He was engaged. Édouard was *engaged*.

All this time, I'd never asked if he was seeing anyone. And he'd never shared.

And here I stood, a complete and utter fool about to tell him the truth about me being pregnant, as if it even mattered to him. Édouard was leaving the next day for Brazil to shoot a film where he would play a sexy dance instructor, and it was clear now that he wouldn't be making the trip alone.

A spurt of rage flowed through me as I thought about all the chances he'd had to tell me about Solange. Then again, I'd had just as many chances to tell him I was pregnant. Even if I *had* told Édouard the truth from the start, I was now certain it wouldn't have mattered.

"Claudia," he said, placing a firm hand on my arm.

I tore away from his grip, unwilling to meet his gaze—the same gaze that had melted me from the inside out these past months. The gaze that, for once, had made me drop my defenses and be vulnerable.

That was over now. *This* was over. It was time to go.

But just as I turned to leave the studio, a jarring pain ripped through my chest, directly underneath the ruby pendant. The pain intensified then soared down through my stomach. I doubled over, hands clasping my tight, round belly, my eyes squeezing shut from the intensity of the pain rushing through me.

"Claudia, what is it? Are you all right?"

I vaguely felt Édouard's hands wrapping around me as my knees buckled and I crumpled to the floor.

Another jolt of pain rattled my insides, and I let out a low whimper. What was happening? I'd lost everything else. Was I going to lose my baby now too?

Édouard's strong voice boomed through the studio, ringing through my ears. "Stay with me, Claudia. Stay with me." He knelt on the hardwood floor, cradling me in his arms.

I will not lose my baby. I will not lose her.

Another frosty draft whipped through the studio, chilling me to the bone, numbing me only slightly to the pain that now rolled through me in waves.

I closed my eyes and felt Édouard's warm breath blowing over my frosty skin, his face only inches from mine.

"Why is it so cold in here?" I whispered, my whole body trembling.

But before I could hear his answer, I saw something in the darkness—it was Édouard's smoky-gray eyes dancing before me. I remembered the way his strong hands had felt on my skin, his warm breath grazing over my neck, his sexy hips and broad chest shifting in tune with mine to the same tango beat we'd danced to just moments before.

Only there was something different about Édouard. His hair was shorter, the lines around his eyes were more deeply pronounced, and his lips were a bit fuller, happier even.

The vision slipped away when another burst of pain ruptured inside of me. I opened my eyes and gasped for breath. Édouard's face—the one I knew—hovered over me, his mouth moving in slow motion, but no sound coming out. The chill that shot through me intensified, spread from my toes up to my chest, my neck, and finally, to my head.

I shivered as Édouard's concerned face distanced from me. Farther and farther away he drifted, his message to me unclear. But by the urgency in his eyes, I knew it was important. No matter how hard I tried to focus though, I couldn't hear him.

I tried to yell, to reach out to him, to tell him that no matter what, he needed to save my baby. But I couldn't because the blackness was quicker. It closed in around me, eerily dark but strangely comforting in its obscurity. And just as the last flicker of light left my sight, I inhaled the strong scent of roses and heard my grandmother's voice whisper in my ear.

"Ruby. *My Ruby.*"

Dancing with Paris

CHAPTER TWO

"Ruby, wake up," a soft, familiar female voice whispered off in the distance.

"Qu'est-ce qui s'est passé?" What happened?

It was a different voice—a man's. And something was odd about the way he spoke. Was he speaking French?

Ruby, Ruby, Ruby.

I went in and out of consciousness as that name flooded my ears, ricocheting through my pounding head.

Then a hand, cool and steady, cupping my chin.

"Ruby! *Lève-toi!*" *Wake up!*

He was definitely speaking French. Was it Édouard? No, Édouard's voice wasn't that demanding or harsh. But I'd understood him. And I didn't speak French.

My brain spun in circles as the skin on my face blazed with heat. I'd never felt so hot in all my life.

Warm breath engulfed me. Where was I? Who was standing over me?

I blinked a couple of times, noticing the weight in my eyelids. It was different. My eyelashes were so long they clouded my view.

The hand on my chin slid up my boiling cheek.

"I'm so hot," I murmured.

But whose voice was that? It wasn't mine.

I opened my eyes fully and focused on the man's, face which hovered only inches from mine. He knelt over me, his brown eyes widening and his thin lips forming words as if in slow motion.

"*Ça va, Ruby? Ça va?*" *Are you okay, Ruby? Are you okay?*

Jean-Pierre. The name soared into my brain as the gruff sound of his voice trickled through my ears. He leaned closer, his breath a mixture of cigarettes and peppermint. I didn't know anyone named Jean-Pierre. Who was this man? I blinked a few more times and refocused on his face—his dark five o'clock shadow and his lips, drawn into a tight line.

Those lips. I knew those lips. As I lay flat on my back, my limbs as heavy as cement, their weight keeping me strapped to the floor, I could almost taste those lips.

"Ruby, you're awake," he said, the corners of his mouth relaxing slightly.

"Jean-Pierre?" I whispered before I could stop myself.

"That's right, baby. Have some water and you can go back onstage."

Onstage?

"Jean-Pierre, she needs a break! We've been rehearsing since six in the morning and she hasn't eaten a thing. You can't keep pushing her like this, not after what happened this week. *Putain.*"

It was the female voice from before, its inflection and feistiness more familiar to me now. But this time, she'd spoken French, hadn't she? And again, I'd understood what she'd said. But how?

I swiveled my head to the left, away from Jean-Pierre, and found a pair of silver strappy heels right in front of my face. The toenails protruding over the edge of the shoes were painted a blood red, and the feet attached to them were small and heavily arched. I worked my eyes up the length of her body to see a pair of legs, short and slim, covered in tan panty hose, then a red sequined leotard with feathers sprouting from the shoulders, and finally a gaudy red-and-silver feathery headpiece.

She knelt down beside me, taking my hand, and immediately the scent of lavender swirled underneath my nose. "We're going to get you something to eat, sweetie. Don't you worry."

I stared into her eyes. They were a crystal green, gleaming in the dim light that surrounded us.

What in the hell is going on?

Suddenly, a vision of me dancing with Édouard flashed through my jumbled head. I'd been planning on telling him the truth about being pregnant. But why hadn't I told him?

And where was he now?

I gazed up at the two concerned faces hovering over me and wondered why Édouard had been replaced with this man and woman who both looked so familiar to me. Why were they calling me Ruby? And why were they speaking French?

Where am I?

"I'm not Ruby," I said, my voice still foreign yet strangely familiar. "My name is Claudia. Do you know where Édouard is? Or my grandmother?" My hand shot up to my neck, but I only felt warm, bare skin where my grandmother's necklace should've been. "And the necklace. Where is it?"

"You see, Jean-Pierre! She doesn't even know her own name. She needs a break. We all do," the woman spouted, hurling daggers at him with her eyes.

Panic seized my chest as I flicked my head toward Jean-Pierre, who towered over me, shaking his head. "After what happened to Gisèle last weekend, no one is in their right mind. Get her some food and water and be back onstage in an hour. We have already replaced the star of the show once this week, and I refuse to do it again. *Merde.*"

Gisèle.

As soon as that name left his lips, the blood drained from my head and the insides of my palms coated with sweat. I closed my eyes, hoping the nausea would leave. Instead, a rush of terror boiled over inside of me.

Why did the simple mention of this woman's name make me want to crawl out of my skin?

My eyes shot open as I reached for the woman with the red feathers in her hair. "Where am I? What's going on?"

A hint of fear passed through her eyes before she glared up at Jean-Pierre. "Bastard," she murmured under her breath. "Come on, Ruby. Let's get you up. You'll feel better once you get some rest."

As she peeled me off the ground, I noticed a crowd of women surrounding me—all of them dressed alike in their low-cut red leotards, feathers, silver high heels, and cherry lipstick. They whispered and stared at me, a few of them with concern etched in their brows, but one of them—a tall brunette with hazel eyes and cheekbones that almost reached her forehead—glared at me so hard I thought my face would break.

I didn't have time to process the ominous feeling that crept into my stomach, because the woman with the familiar green eyes ushered me through the throngs of red and silver and into a messy room lined with mirrors and bright lights and makeup scattered all over the countertops. As my eyes darted frantically around the clutter, a hauntingly vivid sense of déjà-vu suddenly came over me.

I've been here before.

The smell of lipstick, the missing lightbulb over the mirror in the right corner, the racks of skimpy, sequined costumes shimmering before me.

My mind took a mental snapshot of each item, each color, each scent in this room, and for every single one, my brain told me that I'd already touched it, seen it, smelled it.

But how could that be possible?

"Here, doll. Just lie down on the couch and I'll get you some water and something for your head. You'll feel better in no time. Tomorrow's a big night, and we're *not* letting Véronique weasel her way into your role. *La salope.*"

Okay. That was it. I had to let this woman know that although I was having a *major*, inexplicable case of déjà-vu, I did not belong here. I had to get back to my home in San Diego. To my grandma Martine, to my clients, to Édouard… and to my *baby*.

"I have no idea what you're talking about. Who are you? Where am—" I started, but my strange voice caught in my throat as the reflection of a young woman I didn't recognize stared back at me in the mirror.

She wore an outfit almost identical to the other girls, skintight and low-cut, except her leotard was all silver sequins, and a lone red feather stuck out from the soft blonde curls piled atop her head. Her breasts were voluptuous and bursting; her skin as pale as a first snow; her cheeks rosy; her lips full, round, and bathed in crimson lipstick; and her legs long, thin, and toned.

She was undeniably gorgeous.

It was when I gazed into her eyes that my entire body went ice-cold.

She had *my* eyes—the exact same iridescent blue eyes I'd seen each time I'd gazed into a mirror, for all of my thirty-five years as Claudia.

How were *my* eyes in *this* body?

I peered down at my stomach—at *her* stomach—and the air constricted in my lungs as the flat, sequin-covered abdomen confirmed my worst fear.

My baby girl was gone.

I remembered then. I remembered why I hadn't gotten the chance to tell Édouard that I was single. The magazine cover announcing his engagement. The pain that had ripped from my chest down through my stomach.

Lights and sequins blurred around me as I stumbled backward and landed with a thud on the couch.

"Oh, dear. You really bopped your head hard, didn't you?"

I barely heard the woman as she fumbled around the dressing room. How could I have woken up in someone else's body?

Where is my baby? Am I losing my mind?

The woman appeared at my side with a cup of water and some pills. "Here, take these. They'll help with your head."

I pushed her hand away. "No, I can't take pills. I'm pregnant. I'm eighteen weeks along. But something really strange is happening to me. Did I lose her? Did I lose my baby?"

Small lines crinkled around the woman's sea-green eyes, replacing the feistiness I'd seen earlier. "Calm down, sweetie. You haven't lost anyone. And you're not pregnant. I think you just bumped your head a little too hard."

I pushed myself up to a seated position as hot tears filled my eyelids. "I told you, I'm not Ruby. My name is Claudia. And I *am* pregnant. I'm not that girl in the mirror! Tell me where I am. What is going on?" I struggled to breathe the stale, smoky air in the dressing room as I gripped the side of the couch.

The woman reached for my hand. And through my panic, I felt another jolt of déjà-vu...but this time it was one of comfort. I gazed into her green eyes. *Those eyes.* How did I know them?

As if she was talking to a child she said, "My name is Titine. You and I, we grew up in New York City together and we're best friends. We moved from New York to Paris a little less than a year ago, and we dance at the club together."

When I didn't respond to that absurd statement, an exasperated sigh escaped her lips. "Don't you remember any of this?"

"No, I don't. What club? What are you talking about?"

Her brow creased in concern as she pushed a lock of strawberry-red hair off her shoulder. "Ruby, you're a singer and dancer at a famous jazz club near the Latin Quarter called Chez Gisèle."

I'm in Paris?

What is this? Some sort of messed-up version of *The Wizard of Oz*?

Before I could form a coherent response, Titine continued speaking, her eyes revealing a sadness I hadn't noticed before. "And as of this week, after what happened to Gisèle...never mind, we don't need to talk about that tonight. It's been a tough week on everyone. You're the star now, sweetie. And you took a really bad fall onstage. Let's get you upstairs to your apartment and fix you something to eat. I think you're just exhausted."

The dread that had consumed me earlier at the mention of Gisèle's name reared its ugly head once again. "What happened to this Gisèle woman?" I asked. "And why am I the star of the show now?"

Titine squeezed my hand and lowered her glittery eyelids before speaking. "Gisèle *used* to be the star of the show, and she was our closest friend here. But on Saturday night she... she was found dead in her dressing room."

"How did she die?" I asked.

Titine shook her head at me. "You honestly don't remember?"

"Just tell me. Please. What's going on? What happened to Gisèle?"

She let out a weary sigh before looking me in the eye. "Ruby, *you* were one of the first people who found her. And I think you're still in shock."

I swallowed hard and stared back at Titine, my entire body paralyzed with fear.

"When you found Gisèle, her neck was broken…and she'd been shot," Titine continued.

"Did they catch the murderer?"

She bit her lower lip. "Talking about this right now isn't going to help you feel any better."

From the way Titine suddenly avoided my gaze, I knew there was more to this story. And even though I didn't want to acknowledge the possibility that any of this terrifying experience could be *real* by asking another question, I couldn't stop the words as they burst from my lips. "What aren't you telling me?"

Titine stayed silent, her eyes combing the floor for what seemed like hours before she finally lifted her deadpan gaze to meet mine. "The police are investigating you for Gisèle's murder, Ruby…*you* are their main suspect."

Dancing with Paris

CHAPTER THREE

I had to be dreaming. There was no other logical explanation for this insane situation.

If I'd suddenly morphed from a pregnant, straitlaced therapist into this blonde-bombshell performer who was wanted for murder, hell must've frozen over.

I closed my eyes in an attempt to snap myself out of this insane dream, but then I remembered something else about my dance with Édouard.

Before I'd seen the magazine announcing Édouard's engagement and passed out in his arms, Édouard had spoken to me about Paris. This was making more sense now. Of course I would dream about being a dancer in Paris after that conversation. After all, my mind always liked to grab on to the last conversation I'd had, the last song I'd heard, or the last movie I'd watched, then concoct some bizarre dream about it.

But why was everything and everyone so familiar here?

I shook my head and told myself not to overanalyze. If this was a dream—and I was *sure* it was—all I needed to do was go back to sleep within the dream, and I would wake up in my grandma's dance studio in San Diego. I just hoped that when I woke up, my baby would be okay. I had to get back there *now*.

"You said my apartment is upstairs?" I asked Titine, still startled at the sound of this voice, much deeper and more seductive than my own. This was one absurd dream.

She nodded. "Yes, let's get you up there."

Even with her tiny frame, she was able to hoist me up off the couch and support me as she led me to a dark, winding staircase. A familiar musty smell assaulted my nose, and the sound of our heels tapping on the hardwood stairs made me remember walking this exact same path before. With each step, the feeling of déjà-vu grew stronger and the panic returned.

This is only a dream. I'll follow this woman, go back to bed, and when I wake up, everything will be back to normal.

It had to.

Five flights later, we arrived at the top floor, and I found myself gravitating to the tall blue door on the left. Titine reached for the doorknob.

"Does this ring a bell?" she asked as she ushered me into what I was assuming—and *praying*—was my dream-state apartment.

I glanced around the cluttered abode, taking mental snapshots of the rickety black desk in the corner and the piles of newspapers that littered the dusty surface, the pairs of sleek high heels carelessly strewn over the hardwood floors, and the cherry-red scarf draped over the stark white couch. A strong perfume masked the distinct smell of cigarette smoke, and a frosty draft sent shivers up my arms.

I know this apartment. I've been here before.

I leaned against the wall and closed my eyes, telling myself this would all be okay.

This has to be a dream.

But just as I was about to open my eyes, a vision of a man with hair the color of dark chocolate and broad, muscular shoulders appeared in my mind. He stormed toward the window on the far side of the small apartment, and standing there, topless, was the woman I'd seen in the mirror earlier— the woman whose body I was currently *inside*. The man reached for her and kissed her forcefully on the lips as he cupped her breast in his palm, then whispered something in her ear.

My cheeks flushed as I remembered the way his hands had felt on my skin, the way I'd yearned for him to take me. I tried to make out his face, but I could only feel his strong hands, caressing my entire body, their force, their strength unmatched by any other man's.

"Ruby? Are you okay?" Titine asked, snapping me back the present moment.

My eyes jolted open and I forced in a breath, the panic and confusion now settling deep into my core. "I need to lie down. Please, just get me to bed."

She didn't mask the alarm on her sweet, pale face as she ushered me through the living room, her hands wrapped tightly around my shoulders, keeping me from collapsing out of sheer bewilderment.

When I turned the corner into the bedroom, I didn't even have to look to know that the walls would be painted a deep violet and the sheets on the bed would be red.

And they were. *Scarlet* red.

I ignored the flashes of déjà-vu that assaulted me from every direction and instead climbed into bed, desperately hoping for a reprieve from this madness. But just as my head plummeted and I curled up under the red satin sheets, something crinkled underneath the pillow. I slipped my hand beneath the silky scarlet pillowcase to find a small piece of paper folded in half.

I stared at it, knowing somewhere deep in my gut that whatever was written in this note wasn't going to help me get back to sleep.

Just go to bed, I told myself. *None of this is real.*

But my desire to uncover the information hidden inside the paper overpowered my reason.

As Titine left me alone in the bedroom, I unfolded the torn, faded paper. Inside, I found a note scrawled in French in eerie, thick red handwriting. And as I frantically skimmed the words in this foreign language I'd never learned, my brain translated the message directly into English.

MY DEAR RUBY,
I KNOW WHAT YOU DID, AND IF YOU EVEN THINK ABOUT TALKING TO A., THERE WILL BE CONSEQUENCES.
YOURS TRULY,
ℑ. R.

Goose bumps prickled my arms as I squinted to get a better look at the signature. Was it signed *T. R.*? Or *S. R.*? And who was *A.*?

As I gazed down at the hands that held this freaky note, I realized again that they weren't mine. They had long, manicured fingernails painted a deep red, and they were smaller and daintier than my own.

Okay, that was it. I *had* to be dreaming. I wasn't crazy. I wasn't an insane person. These were definitely *not* my hands, and this was definitely not my body.

I needed to wake up *now*. But I couldn't just lie here in this foreign bed and expect it to happen. I had to take action.

I jumped out of bed and ran into the kitchen, where Titine was reaching for a glass in the cabinet. Yanking the glass from her hands, I filled it with cold tap water, closed my eyes, and dumped the chilly liquid over my head.

"What in the hell are you doing, Ruby?" Titine shrieked.

I took a deep breath, peeled one eye open, then the other, but my chest deflated when I realized I was still in this stranger's apartment. Nothing had happened. I was now not only confused and in a complete state of panic, I was also soaking wet, and Titine was staring at me with her mouth wide open.

"Have you lost your mind?" she asked, snatching the glass from my death grip.

"This isn't my life," I announced once more as I paced through the apartment, trying to come up with another method to wake myself up from this insane nightmare. "I'm not Ruby. My name is Claudia. I'm a marriage and family therapist who lives alone in San Diego. And I already told you: I'm pregnant. This life, this body, this apartment—none of it is mine! I just need to wake up," I shouted, hoping the shrieks would snap me awake, but I was still here, in this foreign life, this foreign body, this foreign apartment, with no idea how in the hell I'd gotten here.

"You need to get your act together, Ruby," Titine scolded. "I know you're scared after what happened this week. We all are. We'd all like to conveniently *forget* what's been going on around here, but you can't go around pretending you've lost your memory and saying you're someone else just because you're under investigation for Gisèle's murder! It's only going to make you look guiltier, not to mention insane. Plus, tomorrow night is the biggest performance of our lives, and you cannot mess this up."

Titine charged toward me and grabbed me by the shoulders. "I need this chance just as much as you do, Ruby. This could be it for us. Our way out of these sleazy clubs forever. We could become real stars! But you have to stop this nonsense." She squeezed my shoulders, her lavender perfume engulfing me, her emerald eyes feisty and severe. "Do you understand me?"

I pulled away from her grasp and pointed toward the door. "Get out."

"Excuse me?" she said.

"Please, just leave me alone."

Titine shook her head at me and sighed. "Fine. But your dramatics aren't going to work, Ruby. I'm your best friend, and if I'm not buying it, no one else will either. Please calm down, eat something, and meet me downstairs for rehearsal in an hour." Titine walked toward the door, but before she left, she swiveled back around on her pointy heel.

"Don't even think about spouting off any of this nonsense about being a therapist living in San Diego." The corners of her mouth turned up into a teasing grin. "I mean, if you were going to fake a fall and pretend to lose your mind, couldn't you have come up with a better story than that?"

Ignoring the little voice inside my head telling me that this was all too real and entirely too vivid to be a dream, I raced over to the window, ripped the cherry-red curtains apart, and opened up the French windows to find a small black iron balcony jutting out into the wintry air.

Clutching the ice-cold railing, I climbed onto the tiny plat-form, fully prepared to jump—not to my death, but to my real life back in San Diego.

But instead, I could only gasp.

A scene from the old black-and-white films I used to watch with my grandma Martine played out right before my eyes. Except it was in color. And it was as real as the freezing water still dripping down my face.

Classic cars in cherry red, sky blue, forest green, and jet black chugged along the busy boulevard below, while men clad in black and gray trousers, long overcoats, and dapper black bowler hats escorted women down the crowded, narrow sidewalk. Some of the women wore dark fur coats with matching hats and hand muffs while others kept warm in less-showy peacoats and sleek white gloves. Elegant, colorful scarves adorned their necks, completing that look of pure sophistication that only a French woman could possess.

Cafés and brasseries lined the boulevard, their heated terraces filled to the brim with smoking Parisians leisurely sipping wine, reading the *journal*, or enjoying tiny cups of coffee. Chic clothing stores revealed gorgeous window displays of the most beautiful vintage dresses, hats, and heels I'd ever laid eyes upon. Rows upon rows of black iron balconies just like the one I was currently glued to lined the elegant apartment buildings that surrounded the boulevard.

Sounds of the French language drifted up to my perch on the balcony, my stupefied brain immediately recognizing the words…even though I'd never before spoken French in my life.

I'm really in Paris.

Titine hadn't been lying. But unless a movie crew was shooting a period film right outside my window, this was *not* Paris of the twenty-first century.

I lifted my gaze over the tops of the old stone buildings, past the rows of skinny red chimneys, and caught a glimpse of something I'd longed to see in person all my life—La Tour Eiffel. But as I stared at the top of the majestic tower until swirls of thick gray clouds swallowed it up, a terrifying realization overcame me.

I'd never dreamed in color before. Ever.

And even more shocking was the distinct feeling that I'd stood on this exact balcony, gazing out at this exact view of the Eiffel Tower many times before.

But *not* in my life as Claudia.

It hit me then. Like another shot of ice water to the face. But this time the harsh freeze traveled all the way down to my bones.

I'm really here. I'm in Paris, in some other woman's body, living some other woman's life. A life I remembered. A life in the past.

I'm not dreaming.

Overwhelmed at the magnitude of the situation and utterly confused as to what it all could mean, I hobbled back from the balcony and turned to search the apartment for something that had the date on it. Because at least I knew for sure where I was, but now I had to figure out *when*.

As I riffled through Ruby's clutter, I didn't find a computer or a cell phone or even a television, which confirmed what the old cars and outdated fashions on the street below had already shown me. Then, on the messy black desk in the corner of the living room, I found a copy of *Le Monde*, a French newspaper. And sure enough, just underneath the heading was a date stamped in bold black ink—*lundi 1 décembre 1959*.

Holy shit.

1959?

But I was born in 1977.

How in the hell did this happen?

I stumbled into the wobbly desk chair, then scanned the paper once more just to make sure this was real. That I'd really gone from being pregnant and dancing with Édouard Marceau one minute—in the year *2012*—only to pass out in his arms and wake up in a completely different and absolutely *stunning* body in Paris in 1959 the next.

A bold headline in the center of the front page caught my eye, and my brain—or *Ruby's* brain?—effortlessly turned the elegant French words into English as I skimmed the page.

SISTER OF ESTEEMED SURGEON FOUND DEAD IN THE
LATIN QUARTER

Twenty-six-year-old Gisèle Richard, longtime star of the booming Latin Quarter cabaret club Chez Gisèle, was found murdered in her dressing room after a performance on Saturday night. Survived only by her older brother, renowned obstetric surgeon Antoine Richard, Mademoiselle

*Richard lived a lively and scandalous existence until her
untimely death earlier this week.*

*Replacing Mademoiselle Richard as the lead singer and
dancer at the popular nightclub will be Ruby Kerrigan, a
transplant from New York City who arrived in Paris less
than a year ago. It was this beauty of Irish descent who
reportedly discovered the body of her fellow dancer on the
floor of the deceased's dressing room, with a broken neck and
a bullet wound to her chest.*

*The club's owner, Jean-Pierre Fontaine, refused to comment
on the circumstances surrounding the young performer's
death. Police confirmed a murder investigation is
under way.*

A chill slithered down my spine as an unwelcome image
invaded my mind. I saw a woman lying on the ground, her
neck twisted at an odd angle, her long black hair tangled up
in her feathery red costume, her eyes open but motionless,
and a crimson stream of blood pooling off her chest.

It was Gisèle's lifeless body, just as I'd found her.

Shaking off the sickening memory, I tried not to overthink
the fact that I hadn't even been here for an hour and I'd
already found this new name of mine on the front page of a
major French newspaper, connected to a gruesome murder…a
gruesome murder that I vaguely remembered. But even more
shocking than seeing Ruby's name in print were the tingles
that shot through my body at the mention of Gisèle's brother's name.

Antoine Richard.

I tossed the paper back onto the desk and ran into the
bedroom. I threw the pillows from the bed, and there, crumpled underneath the red satin sheets, was the threatening note
I'd found just a few minutes earlier.

My dear Ruby,

I know what you did, and if you even think about talking to A., there will be consequences.

Yours truly,

Ꝝ. R.

Was the *A.* mentioned in this note referring to *Antoine*? And what *had* Ruby done?

I rushed back out to the living room and riffled through Ruby's mess of a desk searching for more information. Anything that could help me put together the puzzle pieces of Ruby's life, find out who was threatening her, if she had, in fact, been involved in Gisèle's murder, and why I felt so light-headed simply upon reading the name *Antoine Richard*.

But as I flung useless, empty notebooks, papers with meaningless scribbles, and old newspapers from the pile, I began to wonder if this was all in vain...and I even began to wonder if I really had lost my mind.

Maybe my life as Claudia had merely been a figment of my—or Ruby's—imagination. Maybe I had multiple personality disorder or schizophrenia.

Maybe none of my memories—my baby, Édouard Marceau, my life in San Diego—were real. Maybe I really was Ruby and *only* Ruby, and I'd snapped under the trauma of finding Gisèle's body and being accused of her murder. And as a result, I'd created another life to focus on, to hide behind.

But as I threw the last newspaper from the desk in exasperation, my eyes landed on two objects that proved otherwise.

There, lying on Ruby's desk, was *my* red journal, and next to it, the *People* magazine dated December 1, 2012, with Édouard Marceau's and Solange Raspail's faces smiling back at me.

Midnight Train to Paris Excerpt

CITY OF LIGHT BOOK 3

Midnight Train to Paris

PROLOGUE

December 24, 1937
Lausanne, Switzerland

Rosie Delaney stood on the empty platform, gripping the handle of her cherry-red suitcase with ice-cold fingers. She desperately wished that she'd remembered her gloves.

Thick, heavy snowflakes poured from the black winter sky, dusting the tracks in an eerie white glow. Save for the giant clock ticking overhead, the silence in the Swiss train station that night was deafening to Rosie's ears, which had never been so alert.

Despite her nerves, Rosie was certain she'd covered her tracks well. She'd put on quite the show with Alexandre before slipping out of the annual Morel Holiday Gala unnoticed. She'd even resisted the overwhelming urge to say goodbye to the one person she would miss.

Her mother.

Swallowing the lump in her throat, Rosie thought of the lovely sights of Paris and the even lovelier man who would be waiting for her there, in her favorite city, in only a few short hours.

Jacques Chambord.

She'd made the right choice.

Of course she had.

She'd left behind a closet full of shimmering evening gowns, fur coats, jewels, and high heels. Her meager suitcase contained only a few changes of her most practical, modest clothes and a box of letters.

Those letters meant more to her than any jewel-studded closet ever could.

Running her thumb over the newly bare skin on her ring finger, Rosie remembered how suffocating Alexandre's elaborate diamond ring had felt on her left hand. And it wasn't only the ring that had been suffocating.

The memory of him made her forget how to breathe.

If only the train would get here.

A nervous glance at the clock revealed that it was 11:37 P.M.

They would surely be wondering where she had gone by now. She could almost see Alexandre's dark furrowed eyebrows, his beady brown eyes combing the party, searching for his fiancée, his *trésor*, his *poupée.*

Rosie was finished being Alexandre's treasure, his doll.

She was finished keeping him and his elitist, power-hungry family happy.

A train whistle thundered through the night, and adrenaline shot through Rosie's veins as she glimpsed the steam locomotive barreling down the snow-covered tracks.

Only one word soared through Rosie's mind at the sight of the Orient Express on that snowy winter night in the Swiss Alps.

Freedom.

Midnight Train to Paris

CHAPTER ONE

December 23, 2012
Washington, D.C.

Blinding white snow surrounds my sister's silky chestnut locks, her violet eyes screaming out to me.

"Jillian...Jilly. Come! Please come." Isla's delicate red lips form another sentence, but the blustering winds are unforgiving as they swallow up her quivering voice. Iridescent flakes stick to her long lashes, blanketing the tips of her ears, her pink nose, and finally resting atop her high cheekbones, until that beautiful face—the face that I love more than any other—vanishes.

I see only white as I reach for my twin, shouting her name until my throat hurts. "Isla, come back! I'm here, Isla. I'm here!"

Combing through the mountains of snow gathering at my feet, I curse the flakes, which fall in huge, thick clusters, making it nearly impossible to see even a foot in front of me. My feet are as heavy as bricks, stuck to the bitter, wet ground, the snow swallowing them whole.

"Isla!" I scream once more into the white blasts. But a tornado of wind and snow whip around my head until the cold turns my

fingertips blue, my tongue freezing inside my mouth. I cannot scream for Isla any longer.

The freeze travels up to my eyelids, transforming my tears into ice.

I've been crying these frozen tears for Isla our whole lives.

Isla's face appears one last time, a single drop of scarlet blood rolling down her pale cheek.

She doesn't speak this time. Her violet eyes say it all.

"You're too late, Jilly. You're too late."

My eyes pop open, two fresh tears leaking from the corners. Dread coats my stomach as I spot Natalie, my editor, hovering nearby. Disapproval is written all over that scrunched-up forehead of hers as she crosses her bony arms and takes one purposeful step closer.

"Jillian Chambord. In my office. *Now.*"

I lift my head from its resting place between three lipstick-stained coffee mugs, a scattered assortment of pens, and stacks of newspaper clippings. I clear my throat to speak, but my feisty boss is already jetting across the newsroom in her tall black boots.

I tie my wavy brown hair back into a messy bun as I chase her through the bustling offices of *The Washington Daily*, my place of employment and second home for the past six years. The sounds of fingers tapping furiously on keyboards, the ringing of phones, and the exchanging of story ideas comfort me as I ignore the fatigue that threatens to swallow me into a black hole of endless sleep.

What I wouldn't give for just one full night's rest.

But this would be worth the past two weeks of insanity. *It has to be.*

Inside Natalie's upstairs office, which overlooks the madness of the newsroom, she nods for me to sit, but I ignore her, instead pacing in front of her desk. A flurry of snow gathers on the windowsill; her view of the snow-dusted grass on the National Mall leaves an uneasy feeling in the pit of my stomach…but I'm not quite sure why. Maybe it has to do with the fact that I've already had two cups of coffee this morning on an empty stomach. Or the fact that I can count on one hand the number of hours I've slept over the past two weeks.

"Jillian, what is going on with you?" Natalie starts in, tapping a sharp black pen against a stack of rival newspapers on her cluttered desk. "You're running yourself into the ground, and I have yet to receive a page of decent copy from you this week. This isn't like you."

I open my mouth to respond, but a vision of my twin sister's deep violet eyes—exact replicas of my own—forces its way into my consciousness. Sparkling white snowflakes fall around her troubled face, making her blink as red tears pour from her eyes. I stop pacing, gripping the edge of Natalie's desk while I try to erase the scary image from my mind…but I can't shake the notion that I've already seen Isla's face drowning in the snow once today.

"You have five minutes, Chambord. Spill." Patience has never been Natalie's strong suit, but that's what makes her such a damn good editor.

I clear my throat, forcing the eerie image of my sister's snow-covered face and blood-red tears out of my mind. It must've been a nightmare I'd had earlier.

I'm always having nightmares about Isla.

"I'm one step away from breaking the Senator Williams story," I say, feeling the adrenaline pumping through my veins, drowning out that nagging voice in the back of my head, telling me to call my sister back. "You have no idea how huge this is."

Natalie's razor-straight, shiny black hair swishes atop her crisp white blouse as she shakes her head at me. "I told you two weeks ago to leave that story alone. You already covered the murder of those two teenage girls, and you don't have any evidence to link Senator Williams to their death. That anonymous tip you received isn't going to cut it. So unless you have something else for me, cut the bullshit and get back to work." Natalie dismisses me with a flick of her wrist, then turns up the volume on the flat-screen television mounted on her back wall, the constant stream of news blaring through her chilly office.

"I have a source who's willing to go on the record that Senator Williams, *with* the aid of his chief of staff, is funneling money from a child prostitution ring directly into his campaign."

Natalie stops her violent pen tapping, turns the volume back down, then raises a perfectly lined brow at me. "Go on."

"The two teenage girls who were murdered two weeks ago, as you already know from my coverage of their story, were a pair of sisters from Anacostia. They'd been sold into an underground prostitution ring by their mentally deranged mother. What we didn't know at the time was that there's a *third sister*. She was present when the girls were killed that night, and she claims that Senator Williams is not only behind the murders but is also heading up the prostitution ring with the help of his chief of staff."

"*If* this is even true, why has this alleged Sister Number Three waited until now to come forward with her story?"

"Apparently, Senator Williams has his own private room at *Haven,* the high-end gentleman's club where the sisters were murdered, and the three girls had been taken there often, against their will. This particular night, they had a plan to drug the senator and escape, but things got messy. One of them was killed by the senator's security detail, and the other was strangled by a masked Williams. The third managed to get away, but not before stealing a glimpse of Williams without the mask on."

Natalie's stone black eyes show more than a flicker of interest.

"The senator fled the scene immediately, of course," I continue. "Sister Number Three has been hiding out ever since. She's terrified of coming clean because she believes Williams will have her murdered. And based on conversations she overheard at the nightclub between Williams and some of the other men, she's certain he's in cahoots with local law enforcement to keep his record clean at all costs."

"So how in the hell did you find her?" Natalie asks.

"I've been out every night for the past two weeks doing exactly what you've trained me to do—find a story."

"Which means what, *specifically*?"

I don't have the energy to recount the past several evenings I've spent in the slums of Anacostia looking for the third sister or the shady things I've done only to have one face-to-face meeting with her. Nor do I possess the desire to tell Natalie about the late nights I've spent undercover at that vile gentleman's club since it reopened last weekend, meeting equally vile men and trying to dig up dirt on what goes down in those private, expensive rooms...or more specifically, *who* visits them.

"You know I've never played by the rules, Natalie. That's what makes me such a damn good reporter. Who else would've drudged up this insane story for you?"

"One of these days, Chambord, your inability to follow rules is going to bite you in the ass."

Ignoring my boss's ridiculous prediction, I drive my point home. "What matters is that I've reached the third sister, and she's agreed to give us an exclusive with her statement."

"You *do* realize that Senator Williams and his staff have the power to ruin you, me, *and* this entire paper if we go to press with this and even one tiny detail in this girl's outrageous story doesn't check out. You're playing with fire here."

A tired smile graces my lips. "He *and* his chief of staff can throw all the fire they want when they're spending the rest of their lives behind bars, the sick bastards."

"Let's hope that's the outcome," Natalie quips. "Otherwise you've missed three deadlines this week, all for some trashy girl who wants to cash in on a few murders."

I smack the palm of my hand on her desk, startling the smug expression off her face. "She isn't lying!"

"How can you be so sure? Claiming the senator is running a child prostitution ring, funneling money from said prostitution ring into his campaign, and having sex with and *murdering* teenage girls is a monumental accusation. This isn't just another story to advance your career, Jillian. This is the type of story that will end that man's life. Do you understand?"

"I understand perfectly, and I couldn't give a damn about advancing my career. I became a reporter to expose the truth. To expose despicable human beings like Williams."

A heavy silence settles between us, and I wonder if Natalie can smell the hatred that boils in my bones every time I say Williams's name. I wonder if she can see the desperation in my eyes...the desperation I feel to see him and everything he stands for go up in flames.

I don't care if I'm putting my career in jeopardy. For what that perverted man did to Isla, and now to another innocent set of sisters, I would stop at nothing to put him in prison.

I lean over Natalie's desk, narrowing my eyes at her. "In all the years I've worked for you, name one time when I've reported a story that was less than one hundred percent truth."

Natalie doesn't speak. She doesn't speak because she knows I'm right. And she knows she'd be a fool not to allow this innocent girl to come forward with her story so that we can be the paper that brings down such a nasty, demented politician.

"I know I don't have as many years in this business as you

do," I say. "But I know one thing for sure: if we don't break the story first, someone else will."

"Desperate girls looking for money are capable of coming up with the best lies, Chambord. Breaking a story full of meaningless accusations—"

"The girl *isn't* lying," I say once more, feeling a fierce need to protect her. It's a need I can't explain to Natalie. A need I can't and *won't* explain to anyone.

Only Isla will ever know the truth.

"She's coming in today at 3:00 P.M. to go on the record with her statement," I continue. "And she's requested that we notify law enforcement as well. She'll need protection once this story breaks. We'll need someone clean, someone she'll trust. I'm thinking Officer Reynolds. This is the real deal, Natalie. I wouldn't have taken it this far if I weren't absolutely certain."

Natalie stands from her desk. "I assume you've been working alone on this story these past two weeks?"

"Seeing as how you explicitly told me not to follow this lead, yes; I didn't want to drag anyone else in."

"Well, now's not the time to hog all the glory, Chambord. Get Cooper, Martinez, and Mitchell to dig up everything they can on Senator Williams, his chief of staff, and this mysterious third sister. Does she have a name by the way?"

I'd promised the girl I wouldn't tell anyone her real name. Not until she knew she was fully protected and Senator Williams was in custody. She trusted me, and as someone who understood her pain, I would never betray her confidence.

"Well?" Natalie asks, resuming her obsessive pen tapping.

A harsh rapping on the door stops me from having to explain to my editor why even *she* can't be in the know this time.

"Can it wait?" Natalie calls, but Dave, one of our new interns, peeks his head in anyway.

"I'm sorry to bother you, but there's a detective here to see Jillian. He says it's urgent."

Natalie shoots me a questioning glance. "About the Williams story, I suppose?"

A nervous tingle shoots down my spine. Only one of my other colleagues knows that I'm onto this creep. I hadn't even used my usual police contacts to get to the bottom of this story. I knew I'd never get a word out of the third sister if I didn't gain her trust on my own. Plus, her allegation that Williams had someone covering for him in D.C. law enforcement probably wasn't too far off. Powerful, sleazy men like him usually had equally corrupt cohorts working for them all over the place.

So why in the hell is there a detective here to see me?

"Send him in," Natalie says.

As soon as the intern reveals the mystery detective, I feel my stomach tying up in a fit of knots.

Samuel Kelly crosses the room before I can let a word slide past my lips, his cool green eyes and sharp black suit bringing back memories I'd long ago chosen to bury.

He doesn't bother shaking my hand or introducing himself. Instead, the man I'd sworn off forever stops just inches from me, and by the lack of a smile on his rugged face, I'm certain he's not here to reminisce.

"Jillian." Samuel nods at me, his expression all business. "I need to speak with you privately."

The sight of his tall, firm body, his broad shoulders, and those full lips steals my focus *and* my breath in one fell swoop.

I don't trust myself alone with Samuel.

Not today. Not ever.

"Whatever you need to talk to me about, you can say it right here." I cross my arms and glare at him underneath a mask of lust, anger, pain, and love. I *will not* show him the power he still has over me.

Samuel shoots a reluctant glance toward Natalie, then levels his determined gaze at me. "Three women have been reported missing after taking a luxury train traveling through the Swiss Alps, en route to Paris. I'm sorry to be the one to tell you this, but your sister, Isla, is one of those three women."

Midnight Train to Paris

CHAPTER TWO

"That's impossible," I say, ignoring the memory of Isla's snow-covered, blood-streaked face from my terrifying dream.

"Of course that's impossible," Natalie echoes, stalking around her desk, one hand on her hip. "That's impossible because Jillian doesn't *have* a sister."

Samuel raises a questioning brow at me, but I can't respond. All of the breath has been sucked out of my lungs. Could Isla really be missing? In the *Swiss Alps*? And why on earth is *Samuel* the one delivering this news?

"Jillian, is there a room where I can speak with you alone?" Impatience lines Samuel's deep voice as he eyes me suspiciously. He remembers my secrets, my lies. After all, in the end, those secrets were our undoing.

He takes another step toward me, then leans into my ear. "We don't have a lot of time to waste," he whispers.

The familiar scent of his cologne makes it hard for me not to brush my hands over his sexy five o'clock shadow and down the front of his chest, the way I always used to every time I kissed him. It's been six years since I touched Samuel, but the muscle memory is still overwhelming…and maddening.

"Is it true then? You have a sister?" Natalie asks, an incredulous look shooting from her stone black eyes. *Finally,* some emotion.

I nod at my editor, the woman who trusts me to bring her the truth, and only the truth. Except this time, I'd lied about something as basic as having a sister.

And from all of my years reporting for Natalie, I know that she hates liars *almost* as I much as I do.

"Yes, Natalie," I say quietly, feeling suffocated under years of lies. Lies I can't take back now. "I have a sister."

I avert my eyes away from Samuel, furious that he brought this mess into my office, but even more furious at myself for asking him to talk in front of Natalie. He knows nothing about who I've become in the years since we split, yet I'm certain he'll see the same Jillian he knew before—the Jillian who wouldn't tell him the truth about her past.

If only he'd known *why* I couldn't tell him.

"You'll have time to explain later," Samuel says to me. "But right now, I need to ask you a few questions."

I turn back to Natalie, and for the first time since she hired me as an eager college graduate, I can barely look her in the eye.

"Please get the others on the story," I say to her. "I'll join them in the conference room as soon as I'm finished with this. I'm sure it's just a misunderstanding."

I lead Samuel out of Natalie's office without giving her a chance to respond. But as soon as we take a few steps down the hallway, he places a hand on my arm, the mere sensation of his touch sending a shock wave through my core.

"This isn't a misunderstanding," he says firmly. "You know I wouldn't be here otherwise."

The sting in his tone makes me flinch.

My legs feel wobbly as I continue down the hallway in silence, and even though Samuel's crisp black suit is swishing along beside me, I feel totally alone, wishing I had someone to hold me up.

But I don't. I've always only had myself to count on. And today would be no different.

Inside our small conference room at the end of the hallway, I close the door and round the table to reach the window. I need to get as far away from him as I can. I need air.

Outside, the snow is swirling in circles as a harsh wind plows through D.C., rattling the windowpanes, whistling past the building. Is Isla lost somewhere in the snow, crying out for me?

I turn to face Samuel, clutching the windowsill behind me. "What's going on with Isla? And why in the hell is the CIA involved?"

Samuel holds my gaze as he walks around the table, stopping only a few inches from me. I can't help but notice that the sharp white shirt he's wearing underneath his suit *isn't* adorned with a tie. He always hated wearing ties...or rather, he hated anyone *telling* him he had to wear a tie.

That was one of the only things Samuel and I had in common when we'd dated back in college—we never took orders from anyone. I *still* don't.

"I'm not with the CIA anymore." Reaching into his breast pocket, Samuel produces a business card. "I'm a private investigator for an international agency that specializes in finding missing persons, and I've been assigned as one of the lead investigators on your sister's case."

"Isla isn't missing and she doesn't need a fancy investigator to find her. This is just another one of her disappearing acts." I release my death grip on the windowsill and take a step closer to Samuel. This has to be a mistake. Isla can't really be missing.

"When was the last time you spoke with your sister, Jillian?" Samuel refuses to show any emotion on that chiseled face of his, but I remember a different time. A time when his eyes were full of lust for me, filled with a hot, fiery passion. A time when his strong hands owned my body, his lips devouring me until I lost all control.

Samuel was like a drug to me...a dangerous drug that made me lose all my defenses. A drug that made me want to tell the truth about my past.

A past that could never be unraveled.

I shake away the memories. I'd already told Samuel too much. I couldn't have him fishing around about my sister.

"Isla called me yesterday evening," I snap. "She's clearly fine, so you can take that white horse you swooped in on and march it right back out into the snow."

"Did you speak with her?"

I don't tell Samuel that I was inside a drug-infested shack in Anacostia, tracking down the source for my latest story, when Isla's call came through. I don't tell him that it had been the third time this week Isla had tried to get in touch and the third time I'd chosen to put my job first and ignore her call.

Instead, I swallow my guilt and simply say, "No, I missed her."

"Did she leave a voicemail?" Samuel asks.

"I think she might have, but I haven't had a chance to listen to it yet. I'm about to break a huge story, and—"

"Where's your phone?"

"It's downstairs on my desk."

"On my way out, I'll need you to check your voicemail. Any indication Isla may have left you as to what went on yesterday could help us find her. So when was the last time you spoke with her?"

"It was about three weeks ago," I answer, not even sure if my timeline is correct. "She was in Paris, where she's been living off and on for the past two years, and she sounded... good. We didn't talk long—just a few minutes—but she didn't say anything to indicate that something was wrong. I'm sure she just decided to take off and travel without telling anyone. She's been doing that for years." But even as the words exit my mouth, visions of Isla's pale, distressed face cloud my head, those eerie, sparkling white flakes swallowing her up.

Closing my eyes, I wish away the nightmare. The harsh blizzard swirling around her violet eyes. And that teardrop of sizzling red blood.

I know what Isla's blood looks like. I've seen it once before.

As her voice echoes in my mind, her cries pleading for me to come find her, I realize that Isla has never sounded so weak, so terrified.

Not even when death stared her in the face.

Something isn't right.

"Jillian," Samuel says, placing a hand on my shoulder. "I think you need to sit down."

I want to argue, to scream at him that he's wrong, but the image of Isla's petrified eyes won't leave me. Numbness settles into my bones as I slide into the cold black chair.

Something has happened to my sister, and I wasn't there to protect her.

Once again, I'm too late.

"Where is she? Tell me what happened," I demand, my own voice trembling now, terrified to hear the truth.

"Isla was last seen taking the late night Venice Simplon-Orient-Express train through the Swiss Alps," Samuel says, taking a seat next to me. "In the morning, when the train arrived in Paris, Isla wasn't in her sleeping compartment, but her purse and suitcase were left on the train. There were two other girls on the same train last night who didn't deboard in Paris this morning either. And just like Isla, their belongings were left on the train."

"But how is that possible?" I ask. "Were they…were they

taken?" Bile coats my throat as I try to keep from getting dizzy.

"After the train left Lausanne, Switzerland, which is the station Isla boarded from, it stopped briefly at the French–Swiss border because of a mechanical difficulty. Most of the passengers had already retired to their sleeping compartments by that point. We believe Isla and the other two girls were abducted from their sleeping compartments during that stop."

Once again, my breathing fails me as I attempt to wrap my head around the word that flowed so effortlessly from Samuel's lips...*abducted*.

This can't be happening.

"What was Isla doing on that train?" I whisper, wishing desperately that I knew the answer to that question. Wishing that I didn't have to gaze into Samuel's sea-green eyes, the eyes that had always shot straight to the heart of me, past all the bullshit, past all the lies.

"That's what we're trying to figure out," he says. "My team of investigators is already there, working with local law enforcement to interview the other passengers on the train, and a search and rescue team has been called in to comb the area. I'll be meeting them there first thing tomorrow morning."

"Why were you hired to find Isla and the other girls if you're living in D.C.?"

"I don't live in D.C. anymore. Ever since..." Samuel trails off, looking past me and out the window. His eyes glaze over briefly before he clears his throat. "Ever since I took this job, I go wherever they need me to be."

"I'm sorry about Karine," I blurt, knowing full well that it's too late for an apology. That I should've called Samuel when his wife went missing four years ago. I should've called him when my own newspaper covered her abduction...and her murder.

"It's in the past," he says, standing abruptly from the table.

"I'm sorry," I say again, registering the pain flashing through his eyes.

His jaw tightens as he grips the edge of the chair. "I'll do everything I can to find your sister, Jillian. You have my word."

I stand up, remembering all the ways I'd imagined running into Samuel again. Not once did I envision it like this.

"Who hired you?" I ask.

"Frédéric Morel, Isla's fiancé."

This time, it's my turn to grasp onto the chair. "Isla doesn't have a fiancé," I say through gritted teeth.

"And according to her fiancé, Isla doesn't have a twin sister," Samuel says. "Apparently, you haven't been the only one keeping secrets."

A shaky sigh escapes my lips. How could she not have told me she was *engaged*?

"The secrets are going to have to come out now, Jill. I know you've never liked to open up about what happened to you and Isla in the past, but this isn't the time to hold anything back. Not if you want to find your sister alive."

Downstairs, the ringing telephones and tapping computer keys have transformed into nails down a chalkboard. All I can think about is Isla drowning in an avalanche of snow. The business of the newspaper is irrelevant. I have to find my sister.

I lead Samuel to my desk, where I ransack my mess of notebooks and newspaper clippings, searching frantically for my cell phone. With shaky hands, I pull it out from underneath the list of contacts that led me to Sister Number Three in the Williams story.

The thought of Parker Williams's dirty face, of his big, rough hands makes me want to vomit. Isla would want him behind bars too. I would deal with that scumbag later...he could count on it.

One new voicemail.

"I can't listen to this in here," I tell Samuel. "It's too loud. Follow me."

I sling my purse over my shoulder, then lead him out of the suffocating newsroom, through the fancy lobby and out into the blinding white snow. It must be freezing outside, but I don't register the cold as I dial my voicemail. I turn away from Samuel and focus on the peak of the Washington Monument, which is barely visible against the dull white sky and the flakes that swirl all around it.

The streets of D.C. are eerily quiet. Not a single car passes as I wait to hear my sister's voice. The nation's capital has shut down due to the twelve inches of snow that's predicted to dump on the city over the next twenty-four hours, only two days before Christmas.

"Is it her?" Samuel asks, but I hold my finger up to shush him.

"Jillian...oh, Jilly," Isla's voice comes over the line, clear, excited. "You're not going to believe what I've done this time!" She pauses, letting out a devious giggle. "I know we haven't talked in a while...I mean really talked, and I miss you, Jilly. I..." Isla pauses as static rings into the phone, then a loud whistle.

A train whistle.

I brace myself against the cool bricks of the building as Isla's voice returns, softer now. "I have something important to tell you, Jillian. Please call me back. I—I'm..." Isla stops speaking, but the phone doesn't cut off. I can hear Isla's heavy breathing. Then a loud rustling noise followed by a grunt—a *man's* grunt.

And finally the sound of a little girl whimpering.

It's the same whimper I heard when we were only thirteen. The day the gunshots stole any last shred of innocence we had left.

Except this time Isla is twenty-eight-years old. A grown woman. Whimpering like a child because someone has taken her.

The line goes dead, but I've already died inside.

I drop the phone into the inch of snow that has collected at our feet and barely feel Samuel's hands as they reach for me.

You're too late, Jilly. You're too late.

Midnight Train to Paris

CHAPTER THREE

"Where's your car?" I ask Samuel, the urgency of Isla's situation suddenly making it clear what I have to do.

He nods toward a black Escalade parked illegally in front of the building. The windshield is already covered in snow.

I break free of his tight grip on my shoulders, scoop my phone up off the wet ground, and jog toward his car.

"Jillian, I need to listen to that message right now, and then I have to catch my flight to France," Samuel calls after me. "This is no time to mess around."

I turn to face him just as I reach the sleek SUV. "I'm not messing around. I'm coming with you to find my sister."

Samuel shakes his head as snowflakes dust the shoulders of his jet-black suit. "I don't think that's a good idea." He reaches out an open hand, the stern look in his eyes making me want to smack him.

"Give me the phone," he orders.

"Listen, if you don't want me to be involved in this case because of our history together, that's bullshit. This is my sister, Samuel. You know she's the only family I have."

"What about your mother?"

I back up against the door of the SUV, narrowing my eyes

at him. How in the *hell* does he know about her? "We don't
have a mother."

"Really? Because last I checked she was still serving her
life sentence in a Virginia prison. Remember, Jill, I'm an investigator. It's my job to find out everything I can about the
people I'm searching for. You can either help me with that, or
you can obstruct my search for your sister and two other
innocent women. Now give me the damn phone."

I look Samuel square in the eye, then unbutton the top of
my white blouse and slide the phone into my bra. "I'm not
letting you hear Isla's message until you unlock this car and
take me to the airport with you. And then I want you to tell
me everything you know about Isla's supposed fiancé and
anything else you know about her life in France."

"Oh, so *you're* the investigator now?" he quips, eyeing the
opening in my shirt.

"Open the damn car!" I growl.

"Listen, I understand why you want to come. But I know
you, Jill. I know how you operate. If I take you over there
with me, you're going to storm in and try to run this investigation, when you don't have a fucking clue what you're
doing. You didn't know your sister was engaged for Christ's
sake. And the high-profile family who hired me…well, I don't
think it would be wise for me to show up with the sister they
didn't even know existed until a few hours ago."

"Screw that family. *I'm* Isla's family. I clearly know more
about my sister and how *she* operates than anyone else does.
I'm the one who will be able to lead you to her. I know I can.
Just open the car, Samuel."

"In case you're forgetting, someone has abducted your
sister and two other young women from a train. Whoever is
behind this is dangerous, and I can't have you running
around, taking matters into your own hands," Samuel says.
"It's not safe, and I refuse to waste valuable time making sure
you don't get yourself into trouble. This isn't a story you're

breaking for *The Daily*, Jill. We're talking about three innocent lives here."

When I respond by pushing the phone farther into my bra, Samuel shakes his head at me, frustration seeping through his pores. I don't care though. I'm not budging.

"I'll be sending over one of my top investigators this afternoon to question you and get any information that might help us—email correspondence from Isla, information on anyone from your past who may have wanted to hurt your sister—all of it. But right now, I need you to let me listen to that message, then get the hell out of my way so I can catch my flight and find your sister."

I can see that Samuel isn't going to change his mind without a fight. I eye his suit jacket, combing my gaze down the front of his firm chest to his pants pockets. I notice a slight bulge in his left pocket, and that's when I know what I have to do.

Before he can calculate my next move, I grab onto his shoulders and run my fingers up to the back of his hairline, right to the spot at the nape of his neck that used to drive him wild. Then I tip my chin, trying *not* to inhale his intoxicating scent, and press my lips against his.

Snowflakes cover our faces as I brush my lips over Samuel's once, then twice more. I ignore the familiar way he tastes, the heat pulsing through my veins.

By the third kiss, I have what I came in for.

The keys.

I pull away from him, hit the unlock button and run around the front of the car, climbing into the driver's side.

Samuel stands on the sidewalk, his feet planted to the ground, his green eyes glaring at me through the snow. He doesn't run toward me, demanding that I get out of the car. Instead he climbs into the passenger side, runs his hand through his light brown hair, and shakes his head at me as I turn the key in the ignition and press on the gas.

"You haven't changed a bit, Jillian Chambord. Not one bit."

I speed down Constitution Avenue, thankful for the lack of cars on the street and for the Escalade's ability to plow right over the snow.

Samuel's hand suddenly plunges down my shirt.

"Hey!" I say, but he's already retrieved what *he* went in for —my phone.

"Two can play at this game, Jill," he says. His comfortable use of *Jill* momentarily makes me lose focus. He's the only one who's ever called me by that name.

"What's your voicemail password?" he asks.

"1937," I tell him as I speed right through a red light.

"We're not immune to the law. You might want to be a little more careful," he says, punching in my code.

"We don't have time for careful," I quip. "We're going to Dulles Airport I assume?"

Samuel shakes his head. "No, Reagan."

"But, there aren't any international flights out of Reagan."

Samuel holds a finger up to shush me while he listens to Isla's message. He turns the volume up to full blast on the phone, and listens intently. My grip on the steering wheel tightens, my knuckles turning white as I try to block out the sound of her voice traveling through the car.

What was Isla doing on that train?

I gaze over at Samuel as he hangs up the phone. The look in his eyes is determined, strong, hopeful. "This call came in at 6:37 P.M. yesterday, which would've been 12:37 A.M. France time. This confirms that the time of abduction was most likely during the stop they made in the Alps for mechanical problems. This is big, Jillian. This will help us narrow down our ground search."

Samuel pulls out his phone and begins texting while I focus on the snowy road ahead, swallowing the fear that consumes me at the words *abduction* and *ground search*. How can this be happening to my sister? Why haven't I paid more attention to what was going on in her life recently? What if I could've saved her somehow?

I've been so consumed with breaking the Senator Williams story that I…

God, when will I stop lying to myself?

The truth is that most days, it's easier *not* to talk to my twin sister. It's easier not to remember what happened to us and what ultimately tore us apart.

I know Isla feels the same. Which is why I rarely hear from her anymore.

So why did she call me so many times this week? What was she trying to tell me?

A warm hand lands on my shoulder, breaking up my incessant string of worries. "Jillian, your passport. Do you need to stop by your apartment in Rosslyn to pick it up?"

"How do you know I still live in Rosslyn?" I ask.

He sighs. "Jill, just answer the question."

"I have it in my purse. I always carry my passport with me, just in case."

I decide to stop at the next red light, but I don't look at Samuel. I don't want to see the inquisitive, confused expression that I already know has splashed across his handsome face. It's the way he always used to look at me…back when he would ask me questions I couldn't answer. Questions I chose *not* to answer.

The light turns green, and I floor the gas. "Why are we going to Reagan? Are any planes even going to be taking off in this weather?"

"The Morel family—the family your sister was going to marry into—has arranged for a private jet. And yes, that plane will be taking off no matter what. I'll be sure of it."

"A private jet? Are you kidding me? Who *are* these people?"

"The Morels are essentially the French equivalents of the Trumps, except that they come from old money. They own a ton of real estate in Paris and all over France, and they have strong political ties too."

"I see…but I'm still not sure whether I understand why they would go to so much trouble to hire you to find my sister when you're not even going to be in France for the first twenty-four hours of the search. Isn't this a huge waste of time?"

"The agency I work for is the best in the world, Jill. It's made up of people like me—former special agents who've decided to dedicate their lives to finding missing persons. We've given up everything—our homes, personal lives, *everything*—to find these people."

I think about Samuel's wife, Karine, and the coverage my paper did on her abduction and her gruesome murder, and I immediately understand. Samuel is the type of person who wouldn't be able to sleep at night if he knew that what happened to Karine was happening to other women.

"My two partners who are over there right now are both former CIA as well. They've already put a team together to question the other passengers on the train and the Morels. And I just gave the search team a green light, so trust me, no one is wasting any time."

"Fine. But why is this family pulling out all the stops to get *you* over there, Samuel? Why are you one of the leads on this case?" I swerve the car around the traffic circle, the Lincoln Memorial towering to our left, its normally crowded set of stairs completely void of tourists on this harsh winter day.

"In the three years that I've worked for the agency, I've had the highest success rate at finding victims. I've given my life to this career, Jillian. To finding people like your sister.

When I got the call this morning about this case and heard the names of the three women who'd disappeared, I knew I had to take this one."

"Because of me," I say softly.

Samuel nods, the silence of our past together weighing us both down.

I charge over the Arlington Memorial Bridge, the icy Potomac River stretching underneath us. I wonder what it would feel like to jump in the water right now. To be swallowed up into the unbearable freeze. I think of Isla freezing in the snow, lost in the mountains, and for the first time since he stormed into Natalie's office only an hour ago, I am glad it's Samuel here by my side. I'm glad it's Samuel who will be leading the search for my sister.

I won't, in a million years, admit this thought to him though.

"So who are the other two girls that have gone missing?" I ask. "Are they connected to Isla in any way?"

"The three girls all boarded the train from different stops, so it *appears* as if they were chosen at random, but there is a connection we're investigating."

"What is it?" I swerve left onto George Washington Parkway as the windshield wipers bat at the heavy sheets of snow falling from the sky.

"Before I tell you this, you have to promise me you aren't going to leak this back to your editor at *The Daily*," Samuel says, his voice cold. "We're trying to keep the story under wraps to buy us more time to find the girls. Press coverage may tip off whoever is behind this and compromise our search." He pauses and looks away from me. "I've seen it happen before."

"I would never do anything to compromise the search," I say. "And in case this is what you're insinuating, I had nothing to do with the coverage of your wife's story. I would never have—"

"She's dead," Samuel's voice booms through the heated car. "It doesn't matter how those fucking vultures got ahold of the story. Karine is gone."

I zoom down the parkway, letting those words resonate in the air between us. Karine is already gone. I can't let that happen to Isla too.

"I *won't* do anything to mess this up, Samuel," I say. "You have to trust me. Now please tell me the names of the two other girls. Maybe Isla's mentioned them at some point. Maybe I can help."

Samuel types something into his phone and holds up the screen for me to see.

A photo of a young woman with curly brown hair and huge baby-blue eyes stares back at me. "Emma Brooks," he says. "Recognize the name?"

I shake my head. "Sounds vaguely familiar, but I don't think I've ever heard that name from Isla."

"She's the nineteen-year-old daughter of the U.S. ambassador to France, George Brooks."

"Holy shit."

"Which means we only have a day or two tops before every news station in France *and* the U.S. is covering the story."

"A day or two if you're lucky," I say. "An ambassador's daughter was abducted from a train in the Alps. I'm sure Brooks and his family will want to go public with this soon."

"We've already advised them to keep quiet at least until the ground search is underway."

"So what's the connection you need to investigate with Brooks's daughter?"

"We're not sure if Isla and Emma ever met, but we do know that the Brooks family is friends with the Morel family."

"Two high-profile families with tons of money," I say, thinking out loud.

"Exactly. We wouldn't be surprised if we receive a message from the kidnappers asking for millions in ransom in exchange for the two girls."

My foot surges against the gas pedal as I power toward the airport exit ramp. "And what about the third girl? Is she from some other powerhouse French family?"

Samuel punches at the keys on his phone again and produces another photo—this one of a girl with long, silky black hair and striking, almond-shaped eyes. "Francesca Rossi. Italian, twenty-six-years-old. From a moderately wealthy family. No obvious connection to either the Brooks family or the Morel family. She boarded the train in Venice and was sleeping in the compartment right next to your sister."

"Maybe she saw something she shouldn't have, and they took her too. She's probably just collateral damage to the sick bastard who did this."

"To get all three of those girls off the train in the middle of the night without a big commotion, we believe there were at least two, if not three, kidnappers involved."

My stomach curls as I fly down the exit ramp for Washington Reagan Airport.

"Head around this way." Samuel points down a service road that circles the airport. "The plane is waiting for us there."

"Is it going to be a huge problem that the Morel family didn't even know I existed until today, and now I'm boarding their private jet with you?"

"Even if it were a problem, would that stop you?"

Rage soars through my chest as I wonder what the men who took my sister are doing to her right now.

"Nothing would stop me from getting on that plane," I say. "*Nothing*."

Also by Juliette Sobanet

City of Light Series

─────────

≈

ONE NIGHT IN PARIS
CITY OF LIGHT BOOK 1
A NOVELLA

≈

When Manhattan attorney Ella Carlyle gets a call that her beloved grandmother is dying, she rushes to Paris to be by her side, against the wishes of her overbearing boyfriend. Ella would do anything for her grandmother and jumps at the chance to fulfill her dying wish.

But things take a mystical turn when Ella is transported to a swinging Parisian jazz club full of alluring strangers…in the year 1927! As the clock runs out on her one night in the City of Light, Ella will attempt to rewrite the past—and perhaps her own destiny as well.

≈

Dancing with Paris
City of Light Book 2

In Paris, a past life promises a second chance at love.

Straitlaced marriage therapist Claudia Davis had a plan—and it definitely did not involve getting pregnant from a one-night stand or falling for a gorgeous French actor. She thinks her life can't possibly get more complicated. But when Claudia takes a tumble in her grandmother's San Diego dance studio, she awakens in 1950s Paris in the body of Ruby Kerrigan, the glamorous star of a risqué cabaret—and the number-one suspect in the gruesome murder of a fellow dancer. As past lives go, it's a doozy...especially when an encounter with a handsome and mysterious French doctor ignites a fire in Claudia's sinfully beautiful new body.

But time, for all its twists and turns, is not on her side: Claudia has just five days to unmask the true killer, clear Ruby's name, and return to the twenty-first century. To do so, she must make an impossible choice, one that will change the course of *both* of her lives forever.

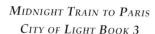

Midnight Train to Paris
City of Light Book 3

When hard-hitting DC reporter Jillian Chambord learns that her twin sister, Isla, has been abducted from a luxury train traveling through the Alps, not even the threat of losing her coveted position at *The Washington Daily* can stop her from hopping on the next flight to France. Never mind the fact that Samuel Kelly—the sexy former CIA agent who Jillian has sworn off forever—has been assigned as the lead investigator in the case.

When Jillian and Samuel arrive in the Alps, they soon learn that their midnight train isn't leading them to Isla, but has taken them back in time to 1937, to a night when another young woman was abducted from the same Orient Express train. Given a chance to save both women, Jillian and Samuel are unprepared for what they discover on the train that night, for the sparks that fly between them . . . and for what they'll have to do to keep each other alive.

Midnight Train to Paris is a magical and suspenseful exploration of just how far we will go to save the ones we love.

~

THE CITY OF LIGHT SERIES: BOOKS 1-3

Save when you read the first three bestselling books in *The City of Light Series* in the newly released omnibus edition!

City of Love Series

SLEEPING WITH PARIS
CITY OF LOVE BOOK 1

Charlotte Summers is a sassy, young French teacher two days away from moving to Paris. Love of her life by her side, for those romantic kisses walking along the Seine? Check. Dream of studying at the prestigious Sorbonne University? Admission granted. But when she discovers her fiancé's online dating profile and has a little chat with the busty red-head he's been sleeping with on the side, she gives up on committed relationships and decides to navigate Paris on her own. Flings with no strings in the City of Light—*mais oui!*

Determined to stop other women from finding themselves in her shoes, Charlotte creates an anonymous blog on how to date like a man in the City of Love—that is, how to jump from bed to bed without ever falling in love. But, with a slew of Parisian men beating down her door, a hot new neighbor who feeds her chocolate in bed, and an appearance by her ex-fiancé, she isn't so sure she can keep her promise to remain commitment-free. When Charlotte agrees to write an article for a popular women's magazine about her Parisian dating adventures—or disasters, rather—will she risk losing the one man who's swept her off her feet and her dream job in one fell swoop?

KISSED IN PARIS
CITY OF LOVE BOOK 2

When event planner Chloe Turner wakes up penniless and without a passport in the Plaza Athénée Hotel in Paris, she only has a few fleeting memories of Claude, the suave French man who convinced her to have that extra glass of wine... before taking all of her possessions and slipping out the door. As the overly organized, go-to gal for her drama queen younger sisters, her anxiety-ridden father, and her needy clients, Chloe is normally prepared for every disaster that comes her way. But with her wedding to her straitlaced, lawyer fiancé back in DC only days away and a French con-man on the loose with her engagement ring, this is one catastrophe she never could have planned for.

As Chloe tries to figure out a way home, she runs into an even bigger problem: the police are after her due to suspicious activity now tied to her bank account. Chloe's only hope at retrieving her passport and clearing her name lies in the hands of Julien, a rugged, undercover agent who has secrets of his own.

As Chloe follows this mysterious, and—although she doesn't want to admit it—sexy French man on a wild chase through the sun-kissed countryside of France, she discovers a magical world she never knew existed. And she can't help but wonder if the perfectly ordered life she's built for herself back home really what she wants after all...

HONEYMOON IN PARIS
CITY OF LOVE BOOK 3

*The sassy heroine of Sleeping with Paris is back! And this time,
chocolate-covered French wedding bells are in the air...*

It's only been a month since Charlotte Summers reunited with
her sexy French boyfriend, Luc Olivier, and he has already
made her the proposal of a lifetime: a mad dash to the altar in
the fairytale town of Annecy. Without hesitation, Charlotte
says *au revoir* to single life and *oui* to a lifetime of chocolate in
bed with Luc. She's madly in love, and Luc is clearly *the one*,
so what could possibly go wrong?

As it turns out, quite a lot...

On the heels of their drama-filled nuptials in the French
Alps, Luc whisks Charlotte away to Paris for a luxurious
honeymoon. But just as they are settling into a sheet-ripping,
chocolate-induced haze, a surprise appearance by Luc's drop-
dead gorgeous ex-wife brings the festivities to a halt. Luc
never told Charlotte that his ex was a famous French
actress, *or* that she was still in love with him. Add to that
Charlotte's new role as step-mom to Luc's tantrum-throwing
daughter, a humiliating debacle in the French tabloids, and
the threat of losing her coveted position at the language
school—and Charlotte fears she may have tied the French
knot a little too quickly.

Determined to keep her independence and her sanity,
Charlotte seeks out a position at *Bella* magazine's new France
office while working on a sassy guidebook to French
marriage. But when Luc's secret past threatens Charlotte's
career *and* their future together, Charlotte must take matters
into her own hands. Armed with chocolate, French wine, and
a few fabulous girlfriends by her side, Charlotte navigates the

tricky waters of marriage, secrets, ex-wives, and a demanding career all in a foreign country where she quickly realizes, she never *truly* learned the rules.

A Paris Dream
City of Love Book 4
A Novella

After the loss of her beloved sister and both of her parents, overworked talk show assistant Olivia Banks sets off on a Paris adventure to fulfill the dreams she and her sister once had as little girls. Olivia only has one day to devote to the City of Light before she must return to her demanding job back in Manhattan. But when she steps out of the cab onto the cobblestoned streets of Montmartre and meets a sexy *boulanger* who wants to help her make all of those dreams come true, Olivia realizes that Paris may have more in store for her than she ever could have imagined.

The City of Love Series: Books 1-3

Save when you read the first three bestselling books in *The City of Love Series* in the newly released e-book boxed set!

City of Darkness Series

~

ALL THE BEAUTIFUL BODIES
CITY OF DARKNESS BOOK 1

~

Take a trip to the dark side of Paris…

After surviving a brutal childhood, Paris-based writer Eve Winters has lived her entire adult life totally under the radar. That all changes one warm spring day when she releases an explicit memoir detailing her dangerous foray into the world of high-end prostitution, and her scandalous affair with a prominent married businessman. The morning of the release, Eve is set to land in New York for her glamorous book launch party…but there's just one problem—she never boarded the plane.

Across the Atlantic, in a Park Avenue penthouse fit for a queen and her millionaire husband…

Acclaimed New York author, writing professor, and socialite Sophia Grayson is all set to attend the book release party of her former student, Eve Winters. *Except...*Eve never shows. When the news travels from Paris that the author has gone missing, Sophia spends the evening reading Eve's shocking memoir. What she discovers in its pages turns her perfect Park Avenue façade upside down and sends her searching for the truth in the one city she'd sworn off forever, the city where she'd locked away her own sordid past and thrown away the key...*Paris*.

True Stories in the City of Love

MEET ME IN PARIS
A MEMOIR

What does a romance novelist do when she loses her own happily ever after? Take a lover and travel to Paris, obviously. Or at least this is what Juliette Sobanet did upon making the bold, heart-wrenching decision to divorce the man she had loved since she was a teenager. This is the story of the passionate love affair that ensued during the most devastating year of Sobanet's life and how her star-crossed romance in the City of Light led to her undoing.

Meet Me in Paris is a raw, powerful take on divorce and the daring choices that followed such a monumental loss from the pen of a writer who'd always believed in happy endings…and who ultimately found the courage to write her own.

I Loved You in Paris
A Memoir in Poetry

In this companion poetry book to her sizzling memoir, *Meet Me in Paris,* Juliette Sobanet gives readers a heartbreaking look into the raw emotions of a romance novelist as she loses her own happily ever after. From the impossible pull of forbidden love to the devastating loss of her marriage, and finally, to rebuilding life anew, Sobanet's courageous poems expose the truth behind infidelity and divorce and take readers on a passionate journey of love, loss, and ultimately, hope.

City Girls Novella Series

CONFESSIONS OF A CITY GIRL: LOS ANGELES
CITY GIRLS BOOK 1

~

When talented DC photographer Natasha Taylor meets alluring investor Nicholas Reyes at her first exhibit, a harmless invitation to join him for a weekend in Los Angeles turns into a passionate love affair that awakens Natasha in ways she never could have imagined.

~

CONFESSIONS OF A CITY GIRL: SAN DIEGO
CITY GIRLS BOOK 2

~

When overworked CIA agent Liz Valentine sets off for a yoga retreat on the gorgeous beaches of San Diego, the last thing she expects to find is love. But when one oh-so-enlightened yoga instructor catches her eye—and her heart—Liz must decide if the loveless life of a secret agent is truly what she wants after all.

∾

CONFESSIONS OF A CITY GIRL: WASHINGTON D.C.
CITY GIRLS BOOK 3

∾

When recent divorcée and famous romance novelist Violet Bell loses her once lustrous career writing happily-ever-afters, a whirlwind weekend in the Nation's Capital with her closest college friend—a sexy British speechwriter named Aaron Wright—could have her wondering if *Mr. Wright* hasn't been right underneath her nose all along...

∾

CONFESSIONS OF A CITY GIRL BOOKS 1-3

∾

Save when you read all three *City Girls Novellas* in one sizzling omnibus edition!

Acknowledgments

To my amazing friends, my loving family, and my dedicated readers. Your love and support keep me writing. Thank you.

About the Author

Juliette Sobanet is the award-winning author of five Paris-based romance and mystery novels, five short stories, a book of poetry, a bestselling memoir, and the screenplay adaptation of her first novel, *Sleeping with Paris*. Under her real name of *Danielle Porter,* she is the author of a new thriller titled, *All the Beautiful Bodies*. Her books have reached over 500,000 readers worldwide, hitting the Top 100 Bestseller Lists on Amazon US, UK, France, and Germany, becoming bestsellers in Turkey and Italy as well. A French professor and writing coach, Juliette holds a B.A. from Georgetown University and an M.A. from New York University in Paris. Juliette lives between France and the U.S. and is currently at work on her next novel. To receive three of Juliette's books for free, visit her website at *www.juliettesobanet.com*. She loves to hear from her readers!

Made in the USA
Middletown, DE
29 November 2020